7/17

THE LAST COWBOYS OF SAN GERONIMO

THE LAST COWBOYS OF SAN GERONIMO

IAN STANSEL

HOUGHTON MIFFLIN HARCOURT
BOSTON ❧ NEW YORK
2017

For information about permission to reproduce selections from this
book, write to trade.permissions@hmhco.com or to Permissions,
Houghton Mifflin Harcourt Publishing Company, 3 Park Avenue,
19th Floor, New York, New York 10016.

www.hmhco.com

Library of Congress Cataloging-in-Publication Data
Names: Stansel, Ian, author.
Title: The last cowboys of San Geronimo / Ian Stansel.
Description: Boston : Houghton Mifflin Harcourt, 2017.
Identifiers: LCCN 2016047296 (print) | LCCN 2017009702 (ebook) |
ISBN 9780544963399 (hardback) | ISBN 9780544963412 (ebook)
Subjects: LCSH: Widows — Fiction. | Husbands — Death — Fiction. |
Sibling rivalry — Fiction. | Fratricide — Fiction. | Revenge — Fiction. |
Horse trainers — Fiction. | California — Fiction. | BISAC: FICTION /
Westerns. | FICTION / General. | GSAFD: Western stories.
Classification: LCC PS3619.T3664 L37 2017 (print) |
LCC PS3619.T3664 (ebook) | DDC 813/.6 — dc23
LC record available at https://lccn.loc.gov/2016047296

Book design by David Futato

Printed in the United States of America
DOC 10 9 8 7 6 5 4 3 2 1

In memory of my sister Kelly –
a real horsewoman

THE LAST COWBOYS OF SAN GERONIMO

ONE

WHAT *are you doing, brother?*
These words clung to the gnarled oak of Silas's consciousness, climbing, nesting, making themselves at home. He set his bones in the driver's seat of his truck and shut the door. Fifty yards away his brother, Frank, lay dead in the dirt, a bullet buried in his chest. Clean heart shot. Silas always had been a hell of a marksman. But now his hands shook and his shoulders petrified and his legs went numb. He looked through the passenger window in the direction of Frank's body but saw only the density of the forest and the darkness of the predawn light.

What are you doing, brother?
After all these years, Frank was gone, put down, but for all the twisted relief—even joy—Silas had expected based on the hundreds of fantasies he'd indulged in regarding this very occasion, he felt no lighter. It wasn't sadness or grief he felt, not regret either, but a deep and frightening nothingness. He kneaded his empty legs, tried to massage some life back into them. On the seat next to him were Frank's Marlboros. Silas picked up the pack, opened the lid, and inhaled the scent of tobacco. Nausea de-

scended upon his gut. He flung open the door and vomited onto the ground, detonating a plume of dry dust.

He went to the trailer hitched to the back of his truck. The horse inside whinnied at the sight of her rider out the window. She wanted to get out, and Silas was ready to oblige her. The back gate creaked open and Silas set a hand on the horse's rump. "All right, girl," he managed. His stomach threatened to erupt again, but he held it off, taking deep breaths of the air in the trailer. This was the scent of his life: horsehair and manure and leather. He led the horse—a fine bay Hanoverian called Disco—out of the trailer, tacked her, and hoisted himself atop. He had bigger horses than this one, but Disco was bright and loyal. She'd never thrown him in the three years he'd been riding her, never once acted out on the lead or tied in the barn aisle. She didn't spook easily and seemed to enjoy a bit of adventure. She'd become his go-to for the annual hunts he put on, and she went up hills and over hedges with zeal. And this was just what he needed.

Leaving the gate down, the driver's side door ajar, and his brother dead in a small clearing, he pressed his legs into his horse's flanks, and the rhythmic drumming of the horse's hooves on the ground made Silas feel something, a familiar jostling of his body, at least. He would take it.

A half hour later he emerged from the woods at the south edge of his own property and took the horse down a dry creek bed, avoiding the town proper just in case any of his few neighbors were up at that odd hour. It wasn't unthinkable. Though residents in the area numbered only a couple hundred, they were an ambitious bunch. Cyclists. Runners. Folks heading up to Point Reyes for the day or down into San Rafael or Sausalito or the city. He edged the south border of the reservoir and took the Indian Hill Road loop northward. At the uppermost finger of the reservoir he dismounted and let his horse drink her fill. Silas unscrewed the lid of his thermos and drank two cups of coffee, black and still steaming in the moist morning. Silas took a moment to meditate on the beauty of the place. The persistent aroma of eucalyptus hung thickly in his nostrils. A wild peacock called from a nearby field. The grass on the hills all around him waved and reflected the sunrise light and shone persimmon orange.

For the past three decades Silas Van Loy had thought of little aside from horses, women, wine, and killing his brother, Frank. In his hazy imaginings of this last occupation's aftermath, there was always more time for the first three. He would kill Frank in whatever way his mind conceived in that particular moment and then continue on with his business, training the yearlings and greenhorns that ambled into his barn, giving lessons, taking students to shows, and then, in the nighttime, visiting local taverns and wine bars and working his cowboy charm on the women, perhaps getting a taker on an invitation back to his trailer. But now that Frank was gone he realized his naiveté. Other than the horse he rode he would have little to do with the gorgeous beasts for the foreseeable future. As for women, riding away from his spread in Nicasio in the wee hours of the morning, the sun making its initial announcements over Mount Tamalpais to the east, he found his desire for them depressed in a way it hadn't been since before his inaugural hard-on at the age of ten, when Alice Carpenter, a homely, squinch-faced girl, lifted her skirt to reveal dust-colored panties bagged around her little buttocks. He was leaving his life behind, his past and his present. The horses, his thirst, and his desires would all have to wait.

In planning this ride, this getaway, he had come to understand how ill-equipped he was. He had tens of thousands of dollars'—perhaps a hundred thousand dollars'—worth of tack and equipment, but did he have saddlebags, something so simple as saddlebags? He finally found a set, hard and dusty and cracked; a rare Western staple in the English riding world of Marin County, they'd been unused for thirty years now. He recognized them as his father's and marveled at how they'd managed to end up there in his tack room all these decades later, how he must have moved them himself without a thought of ever using them. He packed in a few T-shirts and underwear, an extra button-down, a spare pair of jeans, a toiletry set, and a farrier kit for such occasion as Disco's hooves might need a bit of tending. He rolled a sleeping bag and pillow and strapped them to the back of his saddle. In addition to his coffee thermos, he carried a canteen of water and a leather wine bota he'd purchased two decades before in Basque Country and into which he'd funneled a liter of a decent Napa cabernet. For such occasion as he might need a bit of drowning.

He finished his coffee and mounted Disco and continued north, emerging from the bowl of the reservoir, feeling exposed, unmoored in the absence of trees. Crossing Red Hill Road, he was startled by a car coming quick around a bend. It was light enough now, and the car was close enough, that in the split second he looked, he could make out that the driver was a woman, brunette. He wondered what she could see of him. He pressed Disco into a quicker trot and pulled his Stetson lower over his face and directed the horse into a dry, brown channel between two hills. The road seemed to take on some significance, as if it were a boundary line—the first of many—and now that he was past it, he was that much farther away from what had been his life. But Silas also knew that it was just a road, same as any other, and that he was only covering ground. Even if he hadn't the foggiest notion where he was going.

Behind him, the sound of the car passed by and he was left in the shush of the wind purling over the grass.

TWO

WITHIN minutes of her return to the house from the hospital, and before the police came by for their interview, Lena received a phone call. Carly. Old friend.

"Jesus, I just heard," Carly said. "My God, Lena. It can't be, can it."

Lena, exhausted, said, "Yes."

"My God," Carly said again. "What are they saying? I mean, do they have any idea?"

"They don't know." Lena listened to herself talk as if eavesdropping on a casual acquaintance.

"Are they talking about the brother?" Carly knew some of their past. Hell, anybody in the horse world within three counties knew of the trouble between the Van Loy brothers.

"They are."

"Jesus. That guy. And to think I just saw him."

Lena's thoughts clarified, focused. "When?"

"Earlier today. This morning. Do you think I should tell the police?"

Her back stiffened. "Where did you see him?"

"A few miles north of Nicasio. At least I think it was him. I'm pretty sure. He was riding. I saw him cross over Red Hill Road. Seemed to have a good bit of gear with him."

"Back toward Nicasio?"

"No, north. Jesus, do you think I should call the cops?"

"Anyone with him?"

"I didn't see anyone. Lena, really, should I call the cops?"

Lena said, "No." Then lied: "They said they already have him. I'll tell them what you saw."

By the time they came to talk to her, the cops had already theorized that Silas had an accomplice and had left the state. They were in her living room, two uniformed deputies from the sheriff and one in a blue suit who introduced himself as Detective Ortquist. *What an odd name,* Lena thought. She wondered what kind of name it was, its country of origin, all the while marveling at her ability to think of something so trivial right then.

Their speculation on Silas's whereabouts came to Lena in the form of questions: Did she ever hear Silas talk about a specific place he'd like to go? Were there countries he tended to visit? Who were his friends?

This last one was particularly amusing. Aside from women who came around for a while here and there, Silas didn't have friends. As for places he might be, Lena told the cops he'd been to France and Spain and Germany—to buy or sell or show horses —and also that she believed he'd been to Tokyo and perhaps Costa Rica. Lena answered the cops' questions as directly as she could but never told them what she knew: that he was not out of the country nor with an accomplice. The bastard was alone and on a horse.

He had a day's head start, and she was there in her kitchen after having spent fourteen hours being talked at by police and nurses and doctors and family and friends. Not much Lena could do about the bureaucracy of death and dying, so she would have to live with the facts of the situation. But it was in her mind, sometimes at the back, sometimes elsewhere, that he was getting away. Silas. Her husband's brother and murderer.

It was Riley who, later that night, said, "Where do you think he is?"

Riley had driven up from Menlo Park as soon as he heard, with Cindy and the twins following a couple hours later. Back at the hospital, Lena had fallen apart. Crying. Legs giving out. Riley, a good boy, always had been, caught her, said, "It's okay, Mom, I've got you," and she felt his hands, big like Frank's but not callused like Frank's, under her arms, then over her shoulders after she'd regained her footing, and they stayed there in that position, at least in her memory, for the next two hours. But in reality her spell had lasted only a moment. She appreciated Riley's hands on her, but the truth of it was that, after the initial collapse, she did not need them. She could stand perfectly well on her own.

Now at the kitchen table, Lena and her son were dipping significantly into a bottle of Scotch.

Lena said, "Silas? I haven't given it any thought." Not the worst lie she'd ever told, probably, but a lie all the same.

Riley said, "I want to kill him."

She took a drink. "Do you, now."

Cindy and the twins were upstairs, and Riley was speaking idly of murder.

"Don't you?"

"In fantasies, of course. Not in real life." Now, she thought, perhaps this was the worst lie she'd ever told.

"Well, I want him caught. Obviously. The cops must know it was him."

She said, "I imagine so. Unless they're stupider than anyone gives them credit for."

One of the boys cried out upstairs, a protest against bedtime, though it was well past ten. Lena looked at the clock on the range. Nearly eleven. Kid was overtired. Everyone was. Long, terrible day.

Then Riley said, "They'll get him."

Lena said nothing.

Riley said, "I want to see him. In a courtroom. I want to see his face when he gets sent away. I want to see the motherfucker."

She said, "Dear."

"I'm sorry."

"I lost my husband today."

"I'm sorry."

"The only thing I want right now is to sleep."

Riley said, "I'm just . . ." He let his words trail off.

Lena stood, said, "I'm going up." She left an amber puddle in the bottom of her glass and kissed Riley on the top of his head and said, "Don't stay up too long."

❧

She got a few hours of sleep, rose at half past four, regretting that last glass of whiskey, dressed in near silence, then crept past Riley's old room where he and Cindy and the twins slumbered, descended the stairs, and set her feet, one after the other, into the hundred acres of compacted pasture that separated the house from the horses. The night air was wet and penetrating. She cinched the collar of her fleece up to her chin, slipped on the old nylon puffer vest she'd carried from the house, and fished a knit cap from the pocket. By ten the sun would be high and the air warm, but for now the dampness snaked its way through the weave of her jeans.

She switched on only the lights she needed to see. The horses woke and turned in their stalls and angled their heads over the doors and puffed clouds of gray breath into the open corridor. Lena forwent her usual greetings in the interest of stealth and mourning. The horses watched sleepily as she made her way down the aisle. She'd packed her saddlebags and a backpack and sleeping roll the night before and stashed them in the tack room. She hoisted her sturdiest saddle and transferred it to the post outside Pepper's stall. The horse grumbled amiably and hoofed the floor as Lena opened the door to his stall.

"Come on, boy," she whispered, slipping a halter over his ears and running a hand over his wide white blaze. Pepper was a big boy, over sixteen hands, with a quick takeoff. Son of a bitch could hit a gallop like it was nothing and leave your stomach in the dirt thirty yards back. But he was a sweetheart. Now, at this ungodly hour, he offered Lena a hot gust of breath through his nostrils. She clipped on a crosstie, said, "Just a little ride for us this morning."

"Hey," came a voice from the mouth of the barn aisle. Rain.

"Hi," Lena said, trying not to sound alarmed or nervous. "Did I wake you?"

Rain said, "I couldn't sleep."

"No. Nor could I."

"Saw the light come on."

"Sorry about that."

"No. Like I said, I couldn't sleep anyway." She passed a hand over her face and pushed some stray hairs back. A habit she had at the start and end of days. "Riding?"

"Thought I might."

"Early."

"It is that."

"Should I make coffee?"

Lena said, "You should go back to bed."

Rain shrugged. "I'm up now."

She went to the first stall and rubbed the mare's forehead. Rain — Autumn Rain Nelson on her W-9 — had come to the stable at just fourteen, taking lessons and cleaning stalls as partial payment, riding others' horses when owners were away for more than a few days, keeping their horses from getting stiff or lazy. At nineteen she started giving lessons at the summer camps they ran for the rich kids of Marin. Lena supposed she'd liked Rain from the start because she wasn't one of those well-off children of well-off parents. Though they lived, somehow, in this most affluent of counties, her parents seemed to be fairly regular folks — her father a VP at an auto-parts manufacturer and her mother a mortgage underwriter — albeit with enough California hippie in them to name their daughter Autumn Rain. She liked Rain because Rain loved horses enough to want to shovel their shit.

Rain dropped out of San Francisco State halfway through her second year, moved into the apartment above the office, and took over keeping the books. Her parents reluctantly accepted the decision, though according to Rain they still expected her to get over her "horse thing" and return to school — even four years later, when at just twenty-three she basically ran the place, doing everything from giving lessons to ordering feed to making sure the crew was cleaning the stalls and paddocks properly. Rain, Lena had decided long ago, was a real horsewoman. Whether her parents understood it or not, she was in it for life. She couldn't keep away from the animals, instinctually touching them whenever one was near. When a new horse came to the barn, Rain would move to it as if in a trance, running her prematurely red and raw hands over its neck and withers, kneeling and grasping its legs. The animals were her religion. Boyfriends, girlfriends, education, the prospect of a more reliable income—all of these had been laid down and sacrificed to the equestrian gods.

Right then, though, Lena wanted only to get rid of her. The plan had been disrupted and she worried that she might back out if she wasn't gone by daybreak. There is a reason crimes are committed in the dark. Night comes and people lose their minds a little. *Lunacy* is just the right word. But she still had more than an hour, so instead of raising suspicion higher than it already was by her mere presence that early, she changed her tune, said, "Maybe coffee would be nice." Rain disappeared and by the time she returned with two mugs complete with half-and-half and a quarter-spoon of sugar in each, Lena had Pepper fully tacked save for the saddlebags, still stashed in a back corner of the tack room. The sun was inching up toward the horizon, light still just a whispered rumor.

They drank their coffees. Lena pulled on her jodhpurs and tossed her old shitkicker duck shoes back into the tack room. She then urged Rain to try to get a bit more sleep. "It's going to be a busy day and I need to depend on you," she said. "Go on." This last utterance given with the force of a caring boss. An authority. Rain pursed her mouth into a smile, turned back to the apartment, and slipped into the dark. Lena waited a moment. She then finished her preparations—strapped on the saddlebags, twisted herself into backpack straps, cinched Pepper's girth one more notch — mounted, and was off.

In the purple predawn light, she took Pepper through the town of Fairfax. They passed the old movie theater, the restaurants, the deli, the grocery, the elementary school. No one was out yet save for a couple of women, older than her, power-walking. They paid her no mind. How many places were there anymore where the clopping of horse hooves in the middle of a town could elicit so little reaction? She paused in her thinking, her anxiety, her grief, to thank God she lived right there.

Rain would manage the stable for however long it took. She'd done it in the past when Lena and Frank had gone away. Everything would be fine, as though Lena herself were running the day-to-day. The house, at the west edge of the property, the one where Lena had lived with Frank for the past decade, would be fine too. Her horses, her car — they would all remain there as if nothing out of the ordinary were occurring, as if she weren't out stalking her brother-in-law. And if she had to miss Frank's funeral, then so be it. He would understand.

On the far side of town she rode the shoulder of Sir Francis Drake Boulevard up White Hill, excavated granite walls rising on either side of her, walls that within hours would be crawling with sinewy, spiderlike rock climbers. Folks in Marin did so love their recreation. But now the rocks were clear. From the top of the hill, the mouth of the San Geronimo Valley, she would make her way to Nicasio, where her hunt would begin in earnest.

Grief excused all manner of odd behavior. Like taking a horse out for a ride at five o'clock in the morning. Would it follow, then, that she would be forgiven when it came out that she was hunting her husband's killer? No, probably not. That right there, that was a crazy thing to do. A crime. Murder. She wouldn't let her mind skirt the word. She was going out to murder a man. She would track him, thinking with his mind as well as she could, seeing with his eyes. It might take a day, a week. She did not know. She did know that she would be relentless and she would catch him. And when she did, she would fetch the .38 from her pack and shoot him dead.

Only a few cars passed that first morning, their headlights cutting through the dark, illuminating the mist settled on the fields flanking the road. And none of those drivers and passengers would recall seeing a middle-aged woman atop a horse, her eyes ringed with grief but blazing with intent.

THREE

FRANK. The man was a pestilence. Silas used to keep a tally in his head of all the wrongs he'd been done by his brother, but at some point it became useless and impossible. One ill deed morphed into the next. A slight would recall an insult years back. Why bother to differentiate between one and another? It was a sea; what was the use in counting every polluted wave to come along?

Of course there were times that stuck out, specific instances highlighted in his list of grievances. Frank shot Silas, first of all, with a goddamn Colt six-shooter. You don't forget something like that. And this was no childhood playing-with-Daddy's-pistol scenario. This was just twenty years back. Both men in their thirties, and that son of a bitch aimed steady-handed and pulled the trigger, looking to kill. If Silas were a different sort of fellow he might have chalked his survival up to some kind of divine hand. But he wasn't a different sort, and he knew he had just one thing to thank for his pulling through: Frank had always been shit with a pistol.

So that took top billing. But there were others, mostly to do with horses, business. The brothers had waged war on each other since parting as partners when Silas was twenty-nine, just a couple years after their father died and not even a decade after they took over the old stable. Silas didn't like to dwell on their battles too long, for he knew damn well that in the big picture he was no mere victim. But still he ranked Frank's crimes against him as far worse offenses than he'd ever committed. Until now.

He and Frank were born two years apart, Frank the elder. Funny story with Frank: He didn't have a birth certificate until he was in his twenties. Kid was born in the back of a Ford pickup at the side of the road. Their father, Silas Sr., had been rushing his wife, Virginia, to the hospital. This was back in the early 1960s and San Geronimo, where they lived, was about as remote then as the craggy tip of a mountain. But halfway down the hill into town, Virginia says, "No, no, stop the truck, it's here, it's here now, here it comes," and Silas Sr., he tears over to the shoulder and runs around and tosses this big old horse blanket over the bed and goes and pulls his wife out of the truck by her armpits and gets her somehow up on the blanket and she's screaming bloody goddamn murder and by the time he pulls off her undies and pushes her knees up like he must have seen somewhere, the goddamn kid is crowning and Silas Sr., he's thinking, *Oh Jesus, Oh Jesus,* because, one, what he's watching, and two, he's about to be a dad and that whole complex of worry comes crashing in, and then suddenly Virginia is quiet except for these kind of extended groans and sad sighs, and he's in awe of her—how the hell does she know how to do this?—and the head kind of pops through the opening and Virginia says, "Get him, Silas, get him," and he does and by God it is a *him,* and he's a father to a son, and he wipes the kid's mouth out like his wife tells him and the kid is crying, Holy Mother of God, is this kid crying, like Silas Sr. never heard before. Or so the

story went. After a few minutes of dumbfounded silence (and after the confusion of the placenta passing — "Good God, woman,
is there another?" Silas Sr. asked), Silas Sr. says to his wife, "You
okay?" and she pants, "Okay," and then, "Give him here," and
Silas Sr. does and it's only then that he remembers that they're on
the side of the goddamn road, and so he says, "Let's go home,"
and Virginia just nods.

Story continues, Frank was sitting Western before the year
was out. Never went to a hospital, parents never even gave a
thought to registering their child with the federal government.
No one asked for a birth certificate until the taxes on the property
went under his name.

Frank loved this story, told it at every opportunity, thought it
made him some kind of born outlaw, living outside the bounds of
conventions and rules. Gave him what Silas Jr. always thought of
as an unearned swagger. Of course, through the first half of his
life Silas often benefited from his brother's ego. Silas never would
have had the brass, at twenty-one years old, to take over the stable
A to Z, but after a short, intense life of riding and drinking and
smoking, their father was in failing health, and Frank showed no
reservations about assuming control of the place. The old man sat
on a barstool in the sun just outside the south door to the barn,
thinking on the notion a minute. Then he said, "Your grandfa-
ther left me a big old bag of nothing, and I made this out of it.
It ain't much, but it's better than what I got." He pulled on his
Lucky Strike. "I'll be gone soon enough and Ma'll be gone sometime, and the whole shit show'll go on regardless. So you two do
what you want."

Frank took the lead and the boys instituted a plan to rehab
the entire outfit. The elder brother reasoned that there was only

so much money in Western riding, especially in this particular part of the world, so they would change modes, become English. Frank was gleeful about the notion, but for Silas Jr., this meant relearning to ride almost completely. The first time he found himself posting in the saddle, he felt like a sellout. Bit of a queer, even.

"Better than a goddamn redneck," Frank told him that evening. They were in the tack room, a dim bulb illuminating almost nothing, Silas reclined on an old boarder's empty tack box.

"Like riding bareback, these things," Silas said, kicking at a used English saddle Frank had bought earlier in the week.

"You're trying to sit it."

"I been sitting a saddle going on two decades."

"That's the problem."

"This is coming natural to you?"

"Hell no. But neither is being broke, watching these fuckers around here rake it in. Ain't no money in cowboying. Maybe in Pop's day, not today. Not around here."

"We ain't starving."

"That's a low bar you're setting." He clicked the light off and on and off and on. "Do you know how much folks will pay for a fancy horse to take to shows? For some somebody in a white shirt to tell 'em to keep their heels down?"

Later that night, Frank tossed a copy of *The Joy of Riding* onto Silas's bed. He said, "These people don't know the likes of us, brother."

And they didn't, not for a while. Frank and Silas rolled all the barrels out of the old arena and replaced them with jumps. After ten months of rehabbing the old barn, building a new covered arena, trading in nearly all of their old gear for new English saddles, bridles, bits, martingales, and stirrups, all the young men had accomplished was an easy alienating of their old boarders, nearly all of whom shook their heads at the boys' forced trans- formation of their outfit and then made a nearly simultaneous exodus when Frank, without consulting his brother, doubled monthly board fees.

"Your daddy knows about all this, I imagine," one man said to Silas as he loaded his palomino into a trailer. "What's he got to say about it?"

"Frank and I are running the place now," Silas told him, feigning confidence.

"That's clear enough. Watch which way you run it."

Silas stood as the man—one of their last boarders—towed his horse away, out of sight.

Inside the house, Silas said, "Goddamn it, Frank."

His brother sat at the kitchen table and didn't look up from a Dover catalog. "What now?"

"Just lost Jim Glosser. Trailered Atlas away."

"Yeah, he mentioned he was going to do that."

"Glosser's been keeping his animals here since we couldn't reach a fucking stirrup. We're losing everybody, for Christ's sake."

"Seems that way. We'll probably have to remortgage the place."

"Remortgage?"

"Refinance. Whatever they call it."

"More debt, you mean."

"This isn't a something-for-nothing sort of situation."

"We got enough debt."

"Can't get a return without putting something down, and since we got shit to our names right now, we borrow."

"That's called digging a hole."

"That's laying a foundation, Silas."

Silas appealed to his parents. Frank was visiting a stable called Dutton Acres, a sprawling, venerable outfit over in Novato, the aim of the trip being to steal whatever ideas he could from them. So this left Silas and Silas Sr. and Virginia at the dinner table, forks clawing at dark meat. Silas said, "If you two have an opinion about what's happening here, you'd be within your rights to say it."

"Some risks being taken," Silas Sr. said. "That's sure enough."

"I think it's exciting," Virginia said.

"Excitement don't pay the bills," Silas said.

Virginia scoffed. "You don't need to tell us who and what pays the bills."

"I'm just saying it's too much. All at once. You don't tear down the goddamn house while you're living in it."

"You two are partners," Virginia said. "Have you tried talking to him?"

"I don't know," Silas said. "Yeah, I guess."

"You have or you haven't," Silas Sr. said. He set his fork clanging against his plate and took his chicken thigh in hand, got a good bit of meat and fat in his mouth. When he was done chewing he said, "We gave the place to the two of you, but an outfit like this needs one person taking the lead. That's how a thing works. Too many cooks in the kitchen and everything goes to shit." He lit a Lucky and stood. "Good chicken, Ginny," he said. He set a quick hand on his wife's shoulder and then strode into the living room.

Silas and Virginia finished their meals. After, Virginia said, "Frank is the firstborn, and that means something to a man. There's no getting around that. It's the way it's always been. That doesn't mean he doesn't love you." She reached a hand to Silas's wrist. Her fingers were small and felt cold on his skin. Just then Silas wanted nothing more than for the whole operation to fail, to fall apart so utterly that there would be no rebuilding. He swore he would leave horses behind, work the rest of his life drilling holes in some dank factory, if he could only watch his brother's plans burn up in a great display of arrogance gone aflame.

"You two'll work it out," Virginia said, getting up and clearing the table. "Nothing else to do but do."

The next day Frank found Silas outside the arena painting jump poles. "I just got a loan on a new horse today," Frank said. "An Oldenburg. Four years. Ten grand. They're dropping her off tomorrow."

Silas stood in awe of the words, the numbers, which seemed to linger between him and his brother like the smoke of Frank's cigarette. They'd never spent more than five hundred dollars on a horse.

"Knew you'd say no," Frank said in response to the silence. "I also knew you'd come around eventually. The deal couldn't wait for you to catch up."

"Ten thousand dollars."

"Be worth double that when we're done with her," Frank said.

As far as Silas was concerned, this was the end. His brother was a dreamer of big dreams, but reality was reality. Silas could hardly even conceive of ten thousand dollars. The next day, Frank put the Oldenburg in the barn's biggest stall, the one they used for birthing. Silas had to admit to her beauty. Black as oil. Not the biggest horse, a bit under sixteen hands, but powerful, with huge hooves anchoring her body. When Frank brought her to the empty arena and let her loose, Silas saw her move and was won over, captivated. He'd never seen an animal move like that. Dancing, she was. Goddamn dancing. "Look at her," he said.

"That's right," Frank said, hopping up and sitting on the fence next to his brother. "Look at her." They watched the horse for a good ten minutes, watched her run and trot and kick, and when she got that out of her system, they watched her stand there, sniffing at the ground, swishing her tail at flies. Silas wondered if this was anything like what other people felt when they went to church.

Frank broke the silence, said, "You telling me we can't sell this horse for twenty grand or more? A little training? Get some discipline in her? Fuckers'll be lining up. We'll have our pick of buyers. And then we get another one and we train it and we sell it for a pile of money, and then another and another, and in the meantime people see what we can do breaking a horse and they come to see what we can do to teach them to ride and they start boarding here, paying through the nose, and we build more and buy more and sell more and train more and that's how the hell this works, brother."

Silas understood then that his desire to watch Frank fail would go unsatisfied. His brother was right. They would train this horse and sell it for more than Silas had ever imagined possible. They would buy and sell more and the two brothers would become what Frank wanted them to be. Successful. Admired. Known. How much easier it would have been had Frank tossed him off like the dead weight he was. Silas wished he could direct his anger outward, could find some vessel other than himself to carry his disappointment. But, as they would for years to come,

Frank's successes only illuminated Silas's own shortcomings. Silas hated his brother for making him hate himself.

Frank slid off the fence and handed the mare's halter to his brother. "Get her back inside. And next time you want to talk to Ma and Pop about this thing I'm doing, don't. You talk to me or you keep it to yourself."

❦

Silas camped that first night in a shallow valley, under a small brake of poplars, and woke to the sound of Disco's hooves tamping down the dirt just a foot away. Eyes bleary and head throbbing from the wine he'd sucked from that leather teat, he didn't realize for a moment that they were now surrounded by cattle, maybe three dozen. Silas gathered his things and tacked his horse as fast as he could, not wanting to be spotted by any rancher happening by to check on his herd. Disco protested the bit some, not yet having gotten her fill of the field grass. Silas's stomach gurgled and he could feel a bowel movement coming on, but he needed to get away from the camp spot quickly. Didn't want to have to talk to anybody or answer any questions.

Disco moved right along over hills and through valleys, into the rising warmth of the morning, and Silas couldn't help but admire and thank God for the unquestioning nature of these animals. It wasn't stupidity. Far from it. This was a grand intelligence at work, a knowledge that most plots of land were identical. It was people that mistook this place or that for something special. Thinking too much was its own form of stupid, born out of arrogance.

They looped around the backside of the tiny town of Freestone, Silas peering between buildings for any cops on the truncated main drag. He didn't want to stop, but he was already low on supplies. After only a day. He tied Disco to a water-meter pipe in back of the town's store and went in wearing his hat low over his forehead. Inside, he hurriedly filled a basket with bread and sliced roast beef, two cans of vegan chili for nearly seven bucks a pop, three tall cans of a cold coffee drink, and two bottles of water. Silas had already taken a few squeezes from his bota to shake the hangover from his head, and the bladder was nearly empty, so he grabbed two bottles of pinot. He got a pound of carrots and three pounds of apples to tide Disco over until he could refill on grain. The hippie woman at the counter took her time passing the items over the register's scanner and made chitchat about the weather, suggested Silas check out their refillable water bottles, muttered something about chemical leaching, and Silas tried to respond with easy neighborliness and not betray that his heart was pounding away inside his chest.

He and his horse lunched in a green-grassed grove of birch trees two hundred yards off a winding, slope-shouldered road. The plan had been for him to move inland, where fewer people might know him, away from the equestrian world that centered nearer the coast, but there in that stand of trees, he felt a new sense of unease bloom in his gut. The water had always been an anchor, a line defining the edge of the world. Inland he would be adrift. He wouldn't know where to go, and, worse, he wouldn't know where to avoid. So instead, after he fed on bread and beef and one can of cold bean chili, he cut back south a ways and then followed Salmon Creek westward. Midafternoon, Disco drank from Watercress Gulch and they continued on until Silas could nearly hear the insistent pleasure traffic of Highway 1. At this proximity, his breathing eased, but disappointment welled inside.

He hadn't made it even fifty miles from home and already he was backpedaling. Of course, this was why he hadn't let himself come up with a specific plan in the first place. Far easier to justify cowardly navigation when you're moving through a nebulous intention.

Silas got hold of his bota, squeezed the last of the wine into his mouth, turned his horse north, and urged her on.

FOUR

LENA saw the trailer from a hundred yards down Nicasio Valley Road. Her trailer. Parked at the side of the road across from Silas's spread. A strange and disorienting sensation, seeing your own rig where it shouldn't be, outside your husband's murderer's property, no less. She steered Pepper to the gravel shoulder where his steps wouldn't resonate as much. A dun rump, high and muscular, and black tail appeared in the shadow of the trailer. Lena knew the horse. Major. Rain's six-year-old Danish warmblood. Lena had bought him originally and he'd been a school horse for a short time before Rain fell in love with him, had to have him. She'd paid him off in installments over more than two years, during which period Lena and Frank had on several occasions discussed forgiving the debt and just letting her have him. But each time they concluded that he would mean more if the girl had to work a bit harder toward ownership.

Lena came up to the truck slowly, warily, in case she was mistaken, though she knew she wasn't. She said, "What are you doing here?" Startled the girl.

Rain angled her bony elbows out the window of the truck. "I figured this is where you'd start. Figured if I was wrong I'd take Major back. No harm, no foul. But if I was right, then I just might join you."

"What is it you think I'm doing, Rain?"

"I saw the saddlebags in the tack room last night." She nodded toward the gear tied over Pepper's rump. "Those saddlebags."

"Go on back home."

"You think he's making off on a horse, and I think you're right."

"You don't even know the man."

"I know you. I know you wouldn't be out here unless you were certain."

Lena said, "Certainty is for young people and fools."

"The thing I can't figure out is how you're going to find him. He could have gone anywhere."

Lena unhooked her bottle from the saddlebags and took a long drink of water. She said, "Silas Van Loy is a coward and a drunk and a cheat. Plus he's stupid to boot. That's how I'm going to find him." It felt somehow liberating to say this, and she had to tamp down the urge to repeat it again and again, *I'm going to find him, I'm going to find him.*

"So what will you do?"

"Rain, this isn't your concern. Please."

"I can help."

"This isn't fun time. It isn't an adventure."

"I've got my things. I've got a pack and food and water." Rain twisted into the dark of the truck cab, then returned, holding something. She said, "And I've got this." Her hands opened like a tulip to reveal a small silver gun. "My father gave it to me when I moved out to the barn."

"You plan on shooting someone, Rain?"

"No."

"Put it away."

Rain folded a cloth around the gun. She said, "Look what else I have." She held up her phone and the screen lit up, displaying all manner of colorful icons. She tapped at one and a moment later a muffled, nasally voice issued some kind of announcement. "It's a police scanner," Rain said.

"On your phone."

"You can tune in to different departments, listen in."

Lena had to admit that this might be incredibly helpful, and given that the flip phone in her pocket, with its two wings hanging together by wires, was nearly ten years old, she wouldn't have it without the girl.

Rain said, "You all have been good to me. You and Frank both."

"We gave you a job."

"No. It was more than that. And two is better than one. We can cover more ground. Two sets of eyes on the lookout."

"The lookout." Lena suddenly wanted to be anywhere but there, on her horse, having this conversation. She wanted to be in bed, half awake, Frank's warmth covering the short distance between them. What had been commonplace occurrences — those moments when she was smart enough to take notice of what she had — were now fantasies. Frank was gone, and Lena felt more alone than she ever had. And this was why, despite the danger and her instinct to protect Rain, despite the voice inside chiding her for putting the girl in harm's way, she found herself pointing up Nicasio Valley Road, saying, "There's a turnoff up where trail riders park their rigs. Next to the post office. Be ready by the time I get there."

She pressed Pepper into a trot as Rain pulled off the shoulder. Major was out of the trailer and tacked when Lena caught up. The two women made their way north along a well-worn riding trail. The plan, in Lena's head, was to stop in the few towns nearby, ask around. She was half angry at Rain for wedging herself into the search, so she pointedly said nothing about where they were going. More, though, she was angry at herself for being so happy the girl was there with her. They moved at a lively trot through the morning sunlight. On the downward slopes they picked up into a canter.

Carly's Land Rover sat angled on the shoulder of Red Hill Road. She stepped out as the two women approached on their horses. The sun was barely up over the eastern hills of the county, but Carly shielded her eyes nonetheless. "Sweetheart," she said.

The women got closer and Lena said, "You know Rain."

"Of course."

Lena said, "This the spot?"

"Just there," Carly said, pointing up the road. "By that big old tree."

"Cutting right across, then."

"Straight into that little valley."

Lena contemplated the cleft in the earth. "All right," she said.

"Sweetheart, what can I do for you?"

"I'm fine."

"Do they really have him? Silas?"

Lena said nothing and did not look at either of her companions.

"Is she talking to you?" Carly said to Rain.

Rain said, "We're just out for a ride."

"Well, of course I understand that. But this doesn't seem quite right. Lena, you said they had Silas. You said they were talking to him. Is that the truth?"

After a long moment of silence, Rain said, "That's what I heard. Picked him up at his place."

"So you just wanted to see where I saw him?" Carly said to Lena, incredulousness edging her voice.

"I was curious," Lena said finally.

"Curious about what, sweetheart?"

Lena inhaled the scent of eucalyptus and dust in the air. "Curious about where a man goes after murdering my husband."

Lena accepted a long squeeze of her hand and she and Rain said goodbye to Carly, waited until her SUV was out of sight, and rode into the shallow, grassy valley. Over the next hour the air warmed and Lena shed her vest and the two women went along in silence.

Finally, Rain caught up to Lena and said, "He's a good trainer, right? Silas? That's what everybody says."

Lena said, "He knows horses. I'll give the man that."

There was a part of Lena's mind that, a few hours before, had believed that this was not only a chase, but an escape. The house, when she'd returned from the hospital the day before, was filled with Frank. The kitchen retained the faint smell of the bacon he'd made that morning. The book he'd been reading the night before, a Dick Francis mystery, was splayed on his bedside table. He could never find a bookmark. Beard hairs clung to the upper rim of the bathroom sink. The clock in the kitchen seemed to be counting the moments he'd been gone.

But if she'd thought it would be any different out in the open air, astride Pepper, she'd been wrong. The air was his breath. The tree branches were his arms outstretched. The sound of Rain riding behind her was not Rain, but Frank—though it had been so long since they took a ride together on these hills, these trails. His absence surrounded her, crushed her, howled its thunderous silence. When it got to be too much, she urged her horse forward into a canter, but every step Pepper took merely stamped her husband's name into the earth.

Lena and Rain stopped at Soulajule Reservoir and let the horses drink. Lena drank coffee from a thermos and shared two apples with Pepper. They rode on. Midafternoon, Lena's phone began ringing and buzzing with voicemails. Riley, of course. Riley would try to find her, would enlist the cops, get in his little Porsche and drive all over California calling her name angrily into the wind.

"Why'd he do it?" Rain asked. "I mean, do you have any idea?" The two women were crossing through a patch of elms. The trees were wide set but with canopies broad enough to shade the ground and the riders loping across it.

"I don't know. The two of them, they feuded." Lena would not have used that word—*feud*—ten years before. It implied an equality of give-and-take, of aggression and victimhood, and for years she had not perceived the situation between the brothers this way. Not nearly. Frank was no angel, of course, but as far as she was concerned, Silas was the aggressor far more than her husband. Though there were times when she allowed the thought to bubble up from the dark recesses of her mind that there was more to Frank's role in the war and that she simply, consciously or not, turned away when the evidence of it came to light in their otherwise very happy lives.

Soon Rain's phone rang. Lena said, "Ignore it," and the younger woman obeyed without a word. "There's a proper campsite a few miles up. Can't build a fire out on these hills. Too dry. We'd have the cops on us in minutes."

Rain said, "I feel like we're the outlaws."

"We're something close, as far as they'd be concerned."

They made the campsite just as the air was tensing with cold and the sun completed its long descent. A few other groups of people were setting up nearby, laughing and drinking. Lena and Rain hoisted the saddles from their horses, and the animals' sweaty backs steamed in the campfire light. The horses fed on grain and grazed on grass while the women picked packed dirt from their hooves. Rain walked both animals by leads through the grounds to work out their muscles while Lena pierced hot dogs with sticks and peeled the labels from cans of soup and tucked the cans into the fire logs. By the time night fell, the horses were blanketed and the women were packed into their bags.

That night Lena dreamed Frank's wake was underway and the man himself walked through the door in dusty jeans, his old Stetson atop his head. Lena asked him what he was doing there, why he wasn't dead.

"Hell, I was just down the road looking at an Appaloosa," he said.

He pointed out the window and in a field stood a white, winged horse. A Pegasus.

He smiled. Said, "What'd you think, I wasn't coming back?"

Lena looked at him. "I did," she told him, feeling a fool. "I thought you weren't coming back."

❧

There'd been riders in Lena's family going back to her great-grandmother Aileen. Family lore went that when she was nineteen, still then in the family's homeland of England, Aileen rode a horse alone nearly eighty miles from Liverpool to Leeds to see a boy slated to ship off to war. The boy was pretty — with high-set angular features and a tilting smile — and sweet, with a penchant for lyric phrases of love that meant little yet leveled the girl. He died soon after leaving England, but before that Aileen rode her red quarter horse, whose name no one was sure of, back to Liverpool with a love that was so recently and so secretly consummated that she could not conceive of loss, of anything that might fall short of the great tidal wave of love that she was certain would wash over her and her sweet, pretty boy, day after day and night after night for decades to come.

This story was one Lena thought of often as a young woman. It was not the tragic drama at the story's heart that she was taken with, though; rather, it was the picture of her great-grandmother alone atop her horse, traversing narrow trails across windswept English heaths. Lena did not consider herself to be a particularly romantic person, but the figure her great-grandmother cut in her mind was one image she could happily indulge for hours on end.

And it was this story Lena and her mother, Sandra, were recalling the morning they'd first visited the Van Loy stable, trailering their horses on the back of Sandra's AMC Eagle for a show. Lena was twenty-two years old. Frank and Silas had been running their father's place in San Geronimo five years then, and they had built a good reputation as trainers. Still young, with Frank not even approaching thirty yet, but folks were talking. And they knew it, those two. Thought they were a whole new generation of horsemen manifest. So much so that two years before, they'd scheduled their big summer show the same June weekend as the Dutton Acres show. Everyone went to the Dutton show — over a thousand people across the two days. It was one of the primary events on the equestrian calendar. Frank and Silas were aware of the timing, of course. They couldn't not be. But there they went, their first year out, trying to compete. Almost no one went to their event and they lost money and even looked like fools to the few people bothering to notice them in the first place. But then, sure enough, the next year, they did it again. In the prior months, though, they'd amassed some fans. Their barn was full up and the weekend riding seminars they put on sold out regular. A couple dozen folks came out for their show that summer, forgoing Dutton. By the next June, their operation was so popular that Dutton moved their show to September, end of season.

In the field north of the arena, Lena and her mother pulled in and parked amid the flashing chrome of other trailers and trucks. "Big," Sandra said, shielding her eyes and taking in the event.

Lena had her quarter horse Roscoe, whom she'd been riding two years. A good horse. Small and with a wide belly, but smooth, with a surprising agility and height over jumps. Sandra brought a sorrel gelding she'd just bought, a three-year-old. It was his first show.

Lena placed second in their first jumping class. Sandra rode Roscoe in this, too, and took fourth. A joke passed between them —the student becomes the teacher. Some such. A chuckle. Sandra took her gelding in an under-saddle and got blue. A special horse, and Lena liked the way her mother smiled widely as the judge hooked the ribbon on her horse's bridle. Then Lena took another second jumping. A good day for the both of them and they were feeling proud, holding reins out by their trailer and passing a cold bottle of Coke back and forth and wiping their brows, saying "Hi there" when folks went by and nodded, people paying attention, knowing that these two ladies and their horses were doing well this day in June.

"You shoulda gotten blue," a deep voice said.

The two women turned to find a young man, handsome in his anachronistic bolo tie and Stetson. He tipped his hat at them and pushed his sweat-soaked hair back off his forehead before replacing the Stetson.

Lena said, "Oh. Red is a good color for me."

"Well, complexion aside, you got cheated."

"Is that right?"

The man stepped over to Roscoe and set a hand on his rump. "He's a good ol' boy, isn't he."

"He is."

"Nice jumper. I like when you don't expect it by looking at them. They're harder to sell—most people want the ones that'll wow their friends—but a horse like this makes you appreciate what he can do even more. You bought this one?"

Lena nodded.

The man said, "You know horses." Then he motioned toward the arena, said, "One of the judges—guy with longer hair?— he's banging that girl took blue." The man tipped his hat at Sandra. "Pardon my language."

Lena said, "That's none of our business." Though a part of her—a not inconsequential part—felt a welling of outrage. She valued justice, Lena did, and pockets of its absence in the world depressed and angered her.

"If you want to file some kind of complaint with the stable, you'd be within your rights."

She rolled her eyes.

The man said, "I could help you."

"I wouldn't even know who to talk to."

"You could start with me."

"Who are you?"

"I'm Frank Van Loy. I run this stable. I just found out about the judge and the rider. Just now. I wouldn't've let that happen. It jeopardizes the integrity of the event. You clearly outrode her. Blind man could see that. Damn nice ride. So if you feel the need to lodge a complaint, I'll hear it out and do what I can to right the wrong."

Lena looked at him, said, "What could I possibly tell you that you didn't already just say?"

Frank said, after a moment of thought, "Point taken."

Lena fingered the bottom edge of her ribbon. "Anyway, I wouldn't want to do something like that. Like I said, red's a good color for me."

"Shoot. You're a blue rider if I've ever seen one. 'Course you should take lessons with me. Then there'd be no doubt."

He excused himself, tipped his hat again, and disappeared between trailers. "Intriguing," Sandra said. "Seems not to mince words, at least."

"Suppose so."

"Not many men can pull off a hat like that anymore. Not in Marin anyway."

Lena said, "You want me to get his number for you?"

"Don't be cheeky. You should give him yours, though."

"Mother."

Lena had one more class, a jumper, and she took the opportunity to walk the course beforehand. The woman who'd stolen her blue ribbon was there too, counting strides. Lena told herself she didn't care, tried to visualize her ride: Fifteen jumps, highest at forty inches, with two doubles, one off a turn, and a triple. Awkward spacing in that second double. A tough little course all in all.

She rode well. Better than well. Roscoe beneath her adjusted his stride for the second double, got over both cleanly. After that, with just a few fences left, she knew she had it. They took the triple easily. After the last fence the crowd applauded and Lena let out a whoop and clapped Roscoe's neck. On her way out, she saw Frank up in the judges' booth. He stood over the judge with the long hair.

Lena took the blue this time, then found Frank by the concession stand. "Did you do something?"

He was chewing a bite of hot dog. "Do?"

"Up in the booth, with the judges. Did you tell them to give me the blue?"

"Why would I do that?"

"You tell me."

Frank said, "If I told them to give you the blue, it might have been to right the wrong of your last class. Or I might have done it just to show I could. To flirt with you."

"So you did."

"Didn't say that."

Lena pointed at him. "I rode that course cleanly. I rode it better than any other rider in that class."

"I agree with you."

"I don't need you to wield your power or whatever you think you were doing. I don't need you getting cute."

Frank looked down at the gravel ground, then up at Lena. "I was up there asking if any of 'em wanted a Coke."

Lena watched Frank. "Truthfully?"

Frank nodded. He said, "I'm to understand, then, that if I'd done just what you thought I'd done, that would not have been the right way to ingratiate myself with you."

This was one of the stories they told at dinners with friends or at bars after shows. Their origin story. It got laughs, had a happy ending. After all, there they were. But even through years of marriage and after telling the story countless times, Lena still found herself sneaking glances at her husband, trying to discern a signal — some particular steadiness in his eyes, some easy curl to his smile — that would prove once and for all that this story they told wasn't bullshit, that he hadn't, in fact, interfered with the judges' decision, that she had won outright, that she had not, all those years before, been bought with that blue ribbon.

FIVE

THROUGH childhood and adolescence, Frank and Silas rode every chance they got. In the arena at their parents' outfit. Up the trails that led out toward Kent Lake. Down the dusty roads that wound through the San Geronimo and Lagunitas, occasionally passing some early incarnation of the hippie enclaves that would soon dominate so many's perception of the place. They were explorers, the two brothers, bounding on horseback across the crust of this planet. Their world was so small — just a few square miles — and yet it seemed infinite. Silas felt like they were almost a species apart from the rest of the humans on the planet. They understood each other. They understood the sweet smell of fresh manure and the feel of braided reins gripped under fingers. They understood cool, foggy mornings and the hours ahead limitless in promise.

One day when Silas was nine and Frank eleven they'd ridden off up the dusty roads of Lucas Valley. Silas rode a rather dumpy dun mare named, ridiculously, Linda. Frank took a red gelding fox trotter called Stoney. Late afternoon and clouds had come in off the coast, cutting gray across the ultramarine sky, and Frank was saying that they needed to get back home.

"Feeding," Frank said.

It was the boys' job to give the horses in the barn their evening meal, to wing bales of hay over the doors and slip scoops of grain into their buckets. One day not long before, they'd stayed out too long and the old man had had to do the feed; when the boys came in for dinner, no plates occupied their places at the table. The horses don't eat, they don't eat. Silas Sr. was rigid when it came to the horses in their barn, but his sons learned early that this was the only way to care for them. Humans bred the animals, brought them into this world of barns and arenas and stalls, and because of this, humans had to put their needs first. The way it was. The way it had to be.

Silas turned his horse and took the lead down the trail. He was just cresting a small berm and passing a rusted old out-of-use gate frame when Linda spooked, reared back. In his interminable airborne moment, Silas spotted the cause of the commotion —a king snake coiled at the trail's edge, mimicking a rattler. He landed with his shoulder on top of that gatepost. The pain did not come immediately, but when it did, after a second of his being splayed in the dirt, it shot down his arm and up his neck and across his back like nothing he'd ever felt before. It was an extraordinary agony. The snake slithered into the taller grasses, and Linda bolted down the trail, around a corner, out of sight. Frank was off Stoney in a leap. Silas sat up as best he could and Frank said, "Here," and held Stoney's reins out to Silas's good side, and then bounded into the grass. Through the fog of pain, Silas watched his brother scour the ground and then lift his leg and pound a boot into the grass and dirt.

"That son of a bitch's done," he said. "You dying?"

"No," Silas said. "Busted pretty good."

"Hurts?"

Silas nodded, breathing deeply to keep the tears inside.

"We got to get Linda," Frank said, and he shouldered Silas up onto Stoney's back, just off the saddle, then got on himself. Pain ravaged Silas's hunched frame with every step the horse took. After a half hour they found Linda munching grass through her bit in a meadow. Frank dismounted and slapped Stoney's saddle and said, "Slide up there." The older brother rode Linda and led Stoney with reins outstretched. That night the doctor was called to put Silas's shoulder back into place. The old man gave them food even though they'd missed the horses' feeding, but Silas was in too much pain and then too stoned on painkillers to eat. He did remember, though, through the morphine haze, his older brother sitting on the bed opposite his, a dreamy, quixotic grin cut across his face, saying, "I wish I could kill that snake again. I'd go back in time and stomp that son of a bitch over and over if I could." And Silas remembered thinking that the world was full of hazards and unpredictabilities, but the two of them, as long as they stuck together, they'd be safe.

Of course, by the time the old man was on his way out of this world, things had changed. The boys were men. They were running the operation. Virginia had died two years prior, breast cancer. But while her end had been mercifully quick—just two months passing between detection and her burial at Mount Tamalpais Cemetery—Silas Sr. was enduring a prolonged and excruciating demise.

Silas had come to his father's room at the house, one of the two daily visits he dreaded even back when Silas Sr. could still form words, back when Silas had mistakenly thought the situation was at its lowest, back before he understood that the thing eating away at his father's lungs would do far more damage before it was done. Silas couldn't count the number of days he'd figured the old man wouldn't make it through the night, and yet time after time there he was the next morning, his wet eyes pointed at the ceiling, his gaunt chest rising and falling slowly and nearly imperceptibly.

"Frank, he's got brains," Silas Sr. said, swiping a hankie across his spit-glistening mouth.

"He's a smart one, all right," Silas said, capitulating preemptively. Not everything had changed.

"All this with the English, I never thought of it. I'm too old-fashioned."

"You say that like it's a bad thing." He sat on the old man's bed.

"It ain't good. Only people think the old ways are better are sentimental old dipshits. Or people making excuses. Business sense is what your brother's got. Never my strong suit. Not yours either, I guess."

"It's my operation too," Silas said.

"Maybe according to the bank and maybe as far as some of the riders around here see it. But this is his thing he's building. You know that as well as I do. You got horses down, that's for sure. You know those animals. Maybe better than me. Definitely better than your brother. But that isn't brains. That's in your bones. It's running through your veins. It's physical, is what it is. Your brother's built for this world. You and me are just a collection of dumb old cowboy limbs."

The words hit like a blow to the head. Silas had thought of his father's death as the extinction of a species, but now here the old man was telling him, no, *you're* the last one. How humiliated he felt, how foolish. He sat there on the edge of his father's bed, the last dodo, the lone mammoth lumbering across the prairie. Later, in the autobiography he wrote and revised in his head, the story of his life molded and edited to make sense of himself and the world, he had this dialogue with his father down as the moment he knew he would eventually sever himself from his brother and set off on his own. But of course that was simplifying. Storytelling. Truth was that their dissolution was gradual and sometimes numbingly slow. It was in the works for years. Decades. Perhaps from the moment Silas was born and Silas Sr. set his tiny body onto Frank's lap and guided the boy's arms into place to protect the new little one. "You're brothers," Virginia would say whenever they'd fight as boys, as if the word itself was meant to mortar them together, keep everyone from crumbling.

❧

After crossing a meadow, Silas and Disco came to a wire fence that stretched over hills going both north and south. A ways down, Silas eyed a gate, short, not three feet in height. No lock on it, not even a tangle of wire. It would have been easy enough to hop down, kick it wide, and mosey Disco right through. But instead Silas turned his horse and brought her back off the fence some twenty paces and then turned her again. "How about a little jump, girl," Silas said, rubbing the horse's neck. Disco responded with a snorted breath. Silas pressed his boots into the horse's flanks and she leaped forward, picking up speed quickly, adjusting her stride as they approached, and, just as Silas lifted himself up off the saddle, bounding over the obstacle.

"That's it," Silas pronounced loudly as Disco slowed. "That's just goddamned it." He couldn't help the smile that crept across his face. Trotting on, Silas ran his blistered fingers through the coarse hair of Disco's mane.

He saw a man perhaps two hundred yards off making his way down a grassy slope, and the man waved a willowy arm above his head. "Hey there!" the man called. Silas watched him approach from the far side of the field for a good half minute, every second ready to bolt. *Run,* Silas thought to himself. *Go on, go. Give old Disco one good kick and you'll be out of the man's sight, over that ridge, in no time.* But he didn't, and he hated himself for it. Aside from a store cashier, he hadn't talked to another human being in going on three days. Internally, he chided himself for the weakness. Getting lonely. A sorry excuse for an outlaw.

"What are you doing?" the man called.

What are you doing, brother?

"You're on private property," the man said as he got closer. He gestured broadly with his arms. He wore jeans and a white button-down shirt and brown boots and a flopping wide-brimmed hat. His beard was graying and he appeared to be in his early fifties, but his voice was high, like a boy's. "This is all private property."

"Apologies," Silas said. "I was just cutting through."

"I know you were," the man said, offering a slight smile to offset the awkwardness. "That's what everybody's always doing."

"I'll be on my way," Silas said. "I do apologize for any trouble."

"It's no trouble. Just a matter of principle, mostly. Did you happen to close that gate back there?"

"Didn't open any gate."

"Didn't open any gate? How'd you get through, then? If you don't mind me inquiring into your method of breaking onto my land."

"Jumped it."

"This one's a jumper, eh?"

"She does a little of everything," Silas said.

The man's face softened as his gaze took in the horse. "What's she called?"

"Disco," Silas said, then immediately regretted the information.

"Beauty," the man said, a bit wistfully. Silas knew the tone. A horse could do things to a person. Some kind of magic in the air between them.

"You know horses?" Silas asked, prolonging the conversation despite the voice in his head urging him to vacate the situation post-fucking-haste.

"No," the man said. "I've never even been on one, except maybe a pony or two at the fair when I was a kid. And I'm not even sure about that." The man eyed and then pointed to Silas's bota. "What's in that horn of yours?"

"Not much at the moment," Silas said. The man squinted up at Silas. "Little bit of cab left, though. You want some?"

"Is it noon yet?" the man said with a wry grin.

"Somewhere."

The man popped open the nozzle and took a shot from a good five inches. "That's all right," he said.

"You a wine man?"

"A bit of one. Yourself?"

Silas nodded. "Bit."

The man extended a well-worked hand. "Henry Martin."

Silas had come up with a name long before this moment, years before, and that name had woven its way into his fantasies of killing Frank, entered him so deeply that it seemed to be nearly as much a part of him as the appellation given to him by his parents. "Tom Young," he said. It was a good simple name, he thought. A far cry from his own, which he'd always felt was slightly absurd.

"Where are you heading?" Henry asked.

"Nowhere. Just on a wander," Silas returned.

Henry flicked Silas's sleeping roll. "A big one, looks like," he said. Silas nodded vaguely, and Henry seemed to accept this much of an answer as enough. "Where you up from?"

"How do you know I'm up?"

Henry smiled. "You don't strike me as much of a mountain man."

"Sonoma," Silas said.

"That's where you want to be for grape juice. Beats Napa in my opinion. Quality-wise."

"It's an argument a man can make."

"So no particular destination, then?"

"North. Setting camp along the way."

"You got Mendocino Forest just up the road," Henry said. "Decent camping there. Goes up for miles and miles." They were in a valley and green wooded peaks reared up high to the east, west, and north. "You need a lunch?" Henry asked.

Silas had been living the past two days on dry bread and miserly rations of cold cuts. "I wouldn't say no."

"I've got a cellar too," Henry said, "in a manner of speaking."

Silas dismounted and Henry led him and Disco up over a brown-grassed shoulder. As they humped it, Silas looked down the far side and saw a small ranch set in the bowl. A house, a barn, a few sheds and outbuildings. A creek cut through just on the east of the buildings. In the pasture were tall, long-necked animals. Silas furrowed his brow, squinted his eyes. "What the hell you got down there?" Silas asked.

"Llamas," Henry said. "We raise them."

The *we* threw Silas. We. He imagined walking in the door to that little house and finding a woman watching a television screen emblazoned with his face. *Wanted,* it would read just beneath. *Dangerous.* His mind quickly conceived a host of excuses to turn around right then and there, each of them more foolish and unbelievable as the one prior. There was no turning back now. Had to keep moving, steady his breath, step one foot in front of the other, always mindful of the door.

"Don't suppose llamas eat hay," he said.

"Of course," Henry said. He slowed to let Disco come up beside him and then set a hand on her neck. "Some grain too. Yeah, we can get her good and fed."

They passed by the house and the llama pen, and the animals all watched them, their heads turning and then following in unison, and one near the fence uttered a guttural gargle. Disco watched too, out of the corner of her big eight-ball eye. Henry took them to the barn, where there was an unused pen floored with straw. "This'll do," Silas said.

Henry fetched a flake of hay and Disco whinnied at the sound of it. "She'll be okay here?" Henry said, tossing the hay onto the ground.

"She'll be okay here," Silas said. "I thank you."

Henry brought him to the fence line where a few of the llamas dawdled. They licked their mouths with thick tongues and stamped their cloven hooves into the dirt. Their faces resembled a combination of deer and goat and one of those large-eyed Precious Moments cartoons from way back. "Raise these for wool, then?" Silas said.

"We do," Henry said. There was that *we* again. "They get raised for meat, too, but not so much here in this country."

"You ever try it?"

"I did, as a matter of fact, once in Norway. Long time ago, though. Before the farm. Back in a past life."

"Recall the taste?"

"Bit strong, like a very ripe venison, I'd say. I don't think I could eat it now I know the animals. You're a horseman — would you eat horse meat?"

"I believe I'd knock a man out who offered me the meat of a horse."

"I'll keep that in mind," Henry said.

"You said 'we,'" Silas said. "You got a partner here?"

"In a manner of speaking. Maggie and Mira actually own the place. I help tend to the animals. They live there." He pointed a stubby finger at the main house, then pivoted. "I've got that little cottage down the creek."

Silas hadn't even noticed it. Tucked between the creek side and a pair of oak trees was the smallest excuse for a dwelling he'd ever seen. *Cottage* was a stretch. Of course, despite his expanding landholdings, Silas had been living out of a trailer the past fifteen years, so he wasn't in a position to judge.

"Built it myself," Henry said, stepping toward his miniature house. "It isn't big, but it's big enough."

It was dark and cool inside, but Henry tugged at a hanging cord and just above them, two muslin blinds rolled back to reveal skylights that doused the room in sunlight. Aside from the wood trim and a table and small desk, the entire place was white, including the coverings and pillows on a twin bed that seemed to double as a couch. On the far side of the room (which, of course, wasn't so far at all) stood a scaled-down kitchen with a two-burner stove and a sink.

"I've got a couple bottles in my pack," Silas said. "Cab. Nothing special but all right for lunch."

"Save it for your travels," Henry said. He got two glasses and poured a Shiraz from a vineyard down south of Big Sur.

Silas raised his glass. "The hounds," he said.

"How's that?" Henry asked.

"Old toast. To the hounds."

"Is that a horse thing?"

"Something like that."

"To them, then," Henry said.

It was a good wine and Silas wished he were in a position to relax enough to enjoy it. He sat at the table and stretched his neck side to side. It was so bright now in that little house that it hurt Silas's eyes, but each moment he closed them for relief, he saw Frank there on the back of his eyelids.

Henry made chicken salad sandwiches with lettuce and tomatoes, a little lump of potato salad huddled on the outskirts of each plate. The food went quick and filled Silas up. He was no different from a horse when it came down to it; no one was. All just animals trying to get by without dying too early. Food is just about everything, whether it's on a plate or in a trough or straight off some fruiting tree.

He washed the bread and meat and oil down with the wine, and his eyes adjusted to the light and he figured he hadn't had such a simple and pleasant time in God knew how long. The wine was taking effect. He told this man Henry, "Thanks for all this," and hoped those plain words communicated something of the depth of appreciation he felt.

After lunch was finished Henry smiled mischievously and told Silas that he would leave the dishes—of which there seemed to be only two, plus a cutting board—for later. They went outside. "Sonoma," Henry said.

"That's right."

"What do you do there in Sonoma?"

Silas's brain conjured all sorts of occupations—housepainter, mechanic, chef—but none that in this split second sounded plausible. So he told a part of the truth. "I teach horseback riding."

"Been doing that long?"

"Sometimes I feel like I've been doing it since before I was born."

"Maybe you have," Henry said. "A past life."

"You buy into that kind of thing?"

Henry smiled. "Not really. I get why people would, though. It's comforting to think that we get to come back. That this isn't it. One ride around and then it's done."

Silas nodded. If the Buddhists and whoever else were right, what would Frank come back as? A horse? A fly? A blade of grass? Nothing fit. Silas couldn't imagine his brother being anything but his brother. Maybe somehow after all was said and done they'd both come back as themselves. And if so, what would they do different?

Silas and Henry walked along the bank of the dry creek. "It's funny that they call it horse*back* riding," Henry said after some time. "As if there might be some other part of the horse one would ride."

This observation amused Silas. "I never thought about it," he said. "I guess it is funny."

The two men walked and discussed horses and llamas and the weather. Silas tried to offer as few details of himself as he could but still enough that he wouldn't seem withholding. He could see this man Henry loved to talk, once he got going, and it was easy enough for Silas to simply walk and listen. Silas luxuriated in the company. He'd entertained the notion of himself as a hermit, living out the rest of his days in a cabin up in the redwoods, somewhere not far from the coast, fishing and subsisting simply. But he wondered with growing concern if this was possible. He'd been a bachelor all his life, and never one to collect a great number of acquaintances, but there'd always been outlets for his social urges: his boarders and students, vets and farriers, the ladies at the grocery. The past couple days had been the loneliest of his life.

They meandered up the hill and passed by the front of the main house. A door squeaked and a woman's voice rang out. Standing in the doorway was a blonde, maybe fifty years old, nice-looking, with wide hips and high cheekbones. "Oh" was what she'd said, and when Silas turned around she managed "Hello." Silas nodded to her and kept his eyes toward the ground in a manner he hoped wouldn't be perceived as strange.

"This is Tom," Henry said. "Tom, I mentioned Maggie."

"Your outfit here," Silas said, turning back halfway. The sun had arched past its height and was just behind the house, so he had an excuse to hold a hand in front of his face.

"Mine and my wife's," Maggie said. Silas nodded again and continued to nod, hoping this made up for his lack of words at this development. He knew it was foolish and self-absorbed, but even after so many interactions with gay women — the horse world had no shortage—they still elicited a strange twinge of insecurity, as if their orientation were based somehow on their glimpsing Silas and saying to themselves, *Oh, no, no. That's not for me.*

"Tom is riding his horse up north and I found him burgling across the grounds."

"He isn't the first. Honestly, I don't know why you get bent out of shape about it. We don't even use most of it."

"Because it's your land, and private property still means something in this country. Or it should anyway."

"I apologize again," Silas said.

"You we forgive," Henry said, setting a hand on Silas's arm.

"How long are you staying, Tom?" Maggie asked.

"I'll be shoving off momentarily."

But he and Henry kept walking and talking and before he knew it the sky had begun to cloak itself in dusk. Henry invited him to stay for dinner. They'd made it back to Henry's tiny domicile and Silas remained standing in the room.

"Need to find a camp," Silas said.

"You're welcome to stay a night here."

Silas watched the man tidy the dishes still left out from lunch. "Can I ask you something?" Silas said.

"I suppose."

"You queer?"

Henry moved himself to the kitchen, pulled a butcher-paper package from the refrigerator. Silas couldn't tell what was in it beyond a large piece of red meat. His stomach groaned.

"Sometimes," Henry said.

Silas waited for a further explanation. When he didn't get one he said, "You mean you're like a bisexual."

"Exactly like one."

"I always heard that was bullshit. I mean, I've heard you either are or aren't. Gay."

"People like simplicity and definitions. But the way I see it is, if I fuck everybody, what could be more simple."

Silas couldn't help but smile at this. "I'm not, just so you know," he said.

"Knock me over with a feather."

"You ever have anything with either of those women up there at the house?"

"I had a marriage with one."

"No shit," Silas said. "The one I met?"

"Yes. Maggie. We were married for seven years once upon a time."

"And now she's with a woman."

"She is."

"And you're open to either."

"Fuckin' California, right?" Henry said.

"I'm not trying to be rude," Silas said. "You've been very kind to a stranger. I just like to know where I stand with a man."

"You stand in my house, Tom, because I invited you." He flipped the roast onto a pan. "Now, are you interested in dinner and a place to stay?"

"I am, thank you."

"What would you like to drink with dinner?"

"Something red."

Henry looked at Silas askance. "You see me drinking something white with a roast, you can regard that as a sign I've taken leave of my senses."

They ate dinner and sat out front of Henry's cottage enjoying a second bottle of wine, then dipping into a third. The temperature slipped with the sun. In this moment of comfort, Silas felt his lack of a long-term plan wedge its way into his consciousness. He would have to come up with something—a destination, a permanent alias, and a livelihood for when his cash ran out. It was not difficult to force his brain away from thoughts of prison. To imagine that was to imagine himself as some other person living some other existence. But it would not come to that, he thought, grounding his mind in the reality of his life. He would never let that happen.

SIX

THEY crested a hill along a dusty fire route. Lena pressed Pepper into a trot and Rain followed. Here in this desolate part of California, it was nearly possible to believe that the rest of the world had evaporated or slipped away into some ancillary realm. They broke into canters. Down one crushed rock slope, up another. Rolling beige land everywhere.

They'd been listening to the police scanner for a few minutes now and again but were afraid of losing battery power completely. Lena turned her phone off to end the incessant buzzing and chiming of calls, first from just Riley, then the police too. Lena imagined that if she and Rain were to pass a highway, they might see her name illuminated in amber on a board with the words *Missing Adult* and a quick description of her escape vehicle, the steed beneath her.

The first half of the day went by in near silence, the two women threading the valleys, as far as Lena could tell, between Petaluma and Tomales Bay. At noon they stopped and lunched on hard salami and bread and drank water. The horses got grain and apples and carrots and, because they'd found a spot under trees on the shore of a cool, small pond, all the green June grass they could want.

Lena said, "I shudder to imagine what your parents would think about you being out here."

Rain said, "They probably know. Who knows what the cops have put together and who they've talked to."

The girl was right. Lena said, "Jesus, now I feel even worse."

"I'm not a child."

"I know you aren't."

"If it will make you feel better, for the next however many miles we can talk about how I should turn around, but we both know I'm not going to."

Lena was surprised by Rain's tone. Serious. Irritated. A nerve there got hit.

Some minutes later Lena said, "You seeing anybody these days?"

"We don't need to talk about that kind of thing."

"Why not?"

"Because it's trivial."

"I could use some trivial in my life right about now."

Rain grinned and relented. "I see a guy now and then. He'd like it to be more often, but I just don't have the time. Or enough interest, I guess."

"Is he nice?"

"Very nice."

"Good-looking?"

"Sure. Good-looking enough. And smart and basically funny. He's fine. He's better than fine. He's super. But when it comes down to it, most of the time I'm with him I'd rather be riding. Or cleaning tack or mucking out stalls. Sometimes I think I'm still a thirteen-year-old girl, you know, just wanting to be with horses all the time. I mean, yeah, there are certain needs another person can fulfill. A few drinks on the weekend. Some conversation. A bit of a fuck once a month." The girl tore into a piece of bread and did not look at Lena.

"Only once a month?"

"That's what I mean. I feel like I'm supposed to want more of that sort of thing. That year I was in college—everything just felt so stupid. I mean, classes were whatever and it's good to learn, blah, blah, but everything else, all those kids getting high and trying to rub up on each other, it was all so pathetic."

Lena said, "It's experimenting, isn't it. People trying to figure out who they are."

"But I already know," Rain said. "And we only have so much time—" She stopped herself.

That night, with the help of Rain's phone—which, as far as Lena was concerned, was nearly magical in its abilities—the women found another campsite, complete with a proper bathroom and outlets for charging electronics.

Kneeling at a communal fire in the waning twilight, Rain said, "Your mother got you into horses, didn't she?" There were a handful of other campers on the other side of the fire, a blanket across their laps, splashing booze into metal camp cups.

Lena said, "She did."

"She's no longer with us?"

Lena said, "No. She passed on, back when we were still at the old place."

"I'm sorry."

Lena shrugged.

Rain said, "She rode, though."

"As far as I knew as a kid, it was all she ever did." Lena smiled and then felt a pressing on her chest and dropped her mouth. "She got started back in England, near Liverpool, where she grew up."

"I didn't know your mother was English. That explains some things."

Lena looked over. "Such as."

"Little phrases you use. Like the tack room was a mess one day and you said it was all sixes and sevens. I had to look it up."

"She used to say that, my mother."

"There are others. 'Bits and bobs.' I always figured it was a quirk of yours. One time I remember you said Frank was being shirty."

"He could be a shirty bastard," Lena said, letting her voice take on notes of her mother's Merseyside to amuse the girl.

"So what brought your mother here from England?"

Lena said, "My father. What else. He came for school, chemical engineering, at Princeton. They'd just gotten married back over there, so she came with him, of course. Then he got a job in Chicago, so she followed him there. That's where I was born, actually. Father took a job out here when I was two, and so Mother packed up again."

"She trailered horses from place to place?"

"No. No, it was something she did as a girl and then became interested in again later, when I was still a toddler. Father made good money, so it was possible."

"I've never heard you talk about your dad."

"He died when I was young, nine years old. Most of my life it was me and Mum."

Rain said, "You ever think about how different things might

have been? Like, if your parents had stayed in Chicago? Or if your mother hadn't met your father?"

Lena said, "No. I don't think about that kind of thing."

A rustle sounded in the woods behind them. The other campers stopped talking and craned their necks back, and four silhouettes—deer—bounded across the corner of the clearing, then disappeared again into the wood.

"Jesus," Rain whispered. "Do you think this gets boring? To people who live out here? I mean, people must live out here. A few. You think they see that and just think, *Meh.*"

Lena said, "I was in an airport one time—this was in New York, Kennedy—and I was having a drink in a bar and started talking to this woman who turned out to be a big bird watcher. Avid birder, this one. And she said she still got chills when she saw a blue jay. Just a regular old blue jay, after something like thirty years of seeing them."

"That's so cool. That's inspiring."

"It's passion, I suppose."

"Do you ever get bored of horses?"

"No."

"Neither do I."

Lena said, "I know. It's what we breathe. These animals."

A group of three men and one woman, all about Rain's age, shuffled over to the fire. One man with a beard carried a fifth of whiskey. "Hey," the young woman said in Rain's direction. They sat heavily on the ground near the fire.

"Hey," Rain said.

The young woman said, "Community bottle, if you all are interested."

Rain said nothing.

"Go on," the one with the beard said.

Lena said, "Give it here."

In the dim evening light Lena saw the young man's face twist into a self-satisfied smirk, as if it were ever so humorous to corrupt an old lady out here in the wilderness. She poured a couple fingers in her camp cup. She said to Rain, "Have some," and splashed a bit into her cup.

Lena drank her whiskey quickly, the booze heating her throat and chest. Her shoulders, which had been stiffening against the cold, fell slightly. She rose to her feet. "I'm lying down," she said to Rain. To the others, "Thank you for the drink."

"I'll come too," Rain said.

"Stay if you want," Lena said. "Relax."

Rain hesitated, then said, "Okay."

Lena said, "If any of these boys get fresh, just shoot them."

The bearded one snorted and another said, "Damn," and laughed.

Lena leaned down to Rain and whispered, "You have your pistol?" just loud enough for the others to hear.

"Yeah," she said. "I've got it."

The smirks melted and the young people were silent as Lena walked away.

She checked on the horses, both leg-locked and asleep, and then collapsed onto her sleeping bag. The air was getting cooler by the second and here, away from the fire, she felt the chill intensely. She pulled off her jodhpurs and a satisfying ache shook through her feet. She bent her toes forward and back and was about to wriggle into her bag when a voice sounded behind her: "Those your animals?"

She started and twisted to find a man, his feet planted in the dirt but with a torso that leaned forward, as if he were about to topple over. He was heavyset—round at the waist—stubbled, and about her age, though it was difficult to be certain in the darkness. His voice had the character of syrup hardened around the edges.

Lena said, "One of them."

"Something you do, huh, ride horses?"

Lena said nothing to this, as she could not tell if it was a question or a simple note of observation.

The man said, "Been doing it a long time, probably."

"A while. Do you ride?"

The man let out a curt guffaw and slapped his belly. "I look like I ride horses? I'd break a fucker's back."

"You'd be surprised what they can carry."

The man muttered, "Yeah," but didn't offer anything else.

Lena said, "You have a good night." But the man did not move from his spot.

He said, "They used to have cars that started with a crank. Right in the front, you know. A fucking crank you had to turn and turn to get the engine running. Nobody's going to use one of those now, right?"

"I'm not sure I follow." Where was her gun? In the pack just next to her. How long would it take her to retrieve it? The buckle was closed. Two seconds? Three? More? What had been mostly a joke with Rain back at the campfire now seemed like a matter of survival. She hated this man for making her feel fear.

"Nobody's going to drive around in a car you got to crank-start, because why would they? It's stupid. So why is it people still ride around on these big old animals?"

"It isn't about getting places."

The man yanked up the back of his pants. "No, I guess not." He said, "My name's Roger."

What would Frank do to Roger if he could have walked up to this scene? Put him on his fat ass for starters. Lena would say, *Frank, don't,* but she wouldn't mean it and Frank wouldn't listen anyway. Stand over old Roger, he would. *Like scaring women, do you?* he'd say. *Well, I like scaring people too.* Lena, there in that campground, could see her husband toss his Stetson to the grass. Get serious. That lock of hair falling into his face. His lean body seeming to calcify beneath his clothes. She hated how quick his tendency toward physicality could appear and how she too had come to depend on it over their years together. It was how he made sense of the world, and he made sense in her life. Not *of* her life, but *in* it. She knew that had she never met Frank, she would have lived a fine and full existence. She'd probably have married someone else, someone entirely different — nice or mean, tall or short, rich or poor. Someone. And she'd have continued to make what she could of the raw materials of life. But there was no doubt that he made an unexpected sense: his charm, his ambition, his temper, his intelligence, his strength. Even his relationship with his brother. It was all crucial to how she understood him. She'd never before or since met anyone like Frank.

Lena said, "It's been a long day, Roger."

Roger groaned something, a sullen and unintelligible utterance, and then walked away. When, twenty minutes later, footsteps approached, she knew by the soft falls of the heels that it was Rain. The girl settled into her bag, and her breathing eased into barely audible waves. Lena could smell the punch of campfire smoke off Rain's coat and boots, discarded carelessly in the dirt. Lena lay for a long time in the dark, thinking about her husband and thinking about Roger. A small but significant part of Lena wanted the man to return, drunker now, pissed off, looking for that high that bullies get when they find a victim. She wanted him to touch her, grab her, make her fear for her life. And she wanted, with steady hands, to show him the barrel of her gun.

He did not return. And Lena would not recall exactly the muddled thoughts rising and fading in her mind in those last moments before the exhaustion of the day and the intoxication of grief conspired to lure her into sleep. But the next morning, as she and Rain rode away from the dew-damp campground, she saw old Roger sitting alone and slumped at the cold, black fire pit, his shoulders raised into an almost nonexistent neck. He took a drink from a plastic water bottle and then winched the features of his face together and ran his knuckles up his cheek and across his temple. He looked just then like nothing less than a massive hirsute baby woken from his nap and getting up the energy for yet another in a lifetime of tantrums.

❧

The brothers were a novelty in the relatively staid equestrian community of Northern California. Not that the business was any more decent than others; on the contrary, people in the horse world could be a nasty lot — stealing students and boarders from other stables, spreading gossip, cheating buyers. But above this ruthlessness was a thin skin of civility. The Van Loy brothers had no such skin. They cussed and punched fences. They quarreled loudly with feed vendors in the aisle of the barn. They got eighty-sixed from bars. Their students became used to their instructors showing up to lessons limping and bruised. So they were a topic of discussion, those rowdy cowboys who'd somehow infiltrated the rarefied strata of hunter-jumper training. And they might have remained just that, an amusement, if they had not been so damn good at what they did.

Lena imagined that most young people went through a certain process of redefining *family*. You grow up and your world consists of little more than your parents, maybe siblings, grandparents at a stretch. You get married and you love your spouse, but *family* is still those old parents, siblings, grandfolks. It isn't until you have kids that you understand that you've created a new unit, that that old definition of *family* has been altered.

For her and Frank, though, it was more immediate. They didn't have Riley for close to four years after they hitched, but in between they had Silas.

After the wedding, Lena and Frank rented a dime-size bungalow in the hills above San Anselmo while Silas stayed behind at the stable with their father, whose health seemed to dip a bit more toward the inevitable each day. She and Frank came back out to the stable daily, from the early, purple hours of the morning until dusk, which slicked over the forested San Geronimo Valley like spilled ink. Most nights they would be home for an hour, give or take, before her brother-in-law's shape appeared in the frosted-glass front door. He always brought something, a bottle of whiskey or a twelve-pack of Olympia. They drank in those days, all three of them, back when it was still possible to shake off a raging hangover with a couple of Tylenol and a half pot of coffee. The boys, as Lena came to think of them, were woefully clueless about popular culture and would marvel at the records she kept in the hi-fi cabinet. Neither could dance worth a damn, but they played music through the night, and, falling under the power of whatever they were consuming, the three of them twisted and stomped to Springsteen and Journey and Hank Williams Jr.

Years of this. Good nights and bad. On good nights, Silas would pass out on the couch. Lena would cover him with an afghan and then wake the brothers up the next morning with mugs of coffee, which they would collar with little more than a grunt of thanks, the both of them drinking and coughing into their fists, and Frank lighting a cigarette before resuming some previously initiated conversation as if no time had passed.

On the bad nights the boys would get to arguing about this horse or that, this boarder, that student. Frank would tease Silas until the younger brother went silent and it was up to Lena to coax him out of the hole he'd retreated into. Sometimes they got physical, tangling on the hardwood. Lena could never quite tell if it was mock fighting or mock playing, if the anger was the put-on or the goofing was. But they always managed to come out of it with minimal bruising to body or ego. Until the night with the hat.

They were dancing, the lot of them lit on a bottle of Jose Cuervo that Silas contributed, when Frank retrieved his old Stetson from the hook in the bedroom. He looked good in that hat and he could be a vain man and he came shimmying up to Lena with one of those lusty grins Lena pretended to be immune to. They danced, Frank's hand pressed to the small of Lena's back, his face aimed down at her, mouth pursed into something between a grimace and a smirk. This routine might have seemed comical but for the fact that Frank never broke, never let up, never gave any indication that he would ever want to be anywhere but right there swaying with his wife, and his earnestness in these moments was so utterly goddamn sexy.

The fun would not last. Silas tossed back a shot, sidled up on exaggerated tiptoes, and snatched the hat off his brother's head.

"Sneaky fucker," Frank said, breaking away from Lena and going after Silas, who, now wearing the hat, had taken refuge on the far side of the dining table. Frank said, "Gimme back my hat, you thief."

"I think I'll hang on to it for a while," Silas said. "It's a good fit."

The two of them circled the table, Lena retreating to the edge of the small living room, watching half in amusement at their boyishness, half in fear that the play might turn to something else. Which of course it did, quickly.

Frank caught his little brother by the shoulder and after an initial scuffle, they both went down hard. Frank reclaimed his hat, but Silas rolled onto his brother, and their smiles twisted into snarls as Silas got a jab into Frank's rib and Frank landed a shot to Silas's side and then wrapped his little brother in a headlock, the sight of which made Lena's airway feel constricted.

"Stop it, you idiots," Lena said, and after another moment—a point being proven—Frank let Silas go.

"You don't know when a joke stops being funny, brother," Frank said to Silas.

"And you don't deserve a hat like that."

"Fuck you. What the fuck is that supposed to mean?"

And then the waters of anger or resentment or jealousy— Lena didn't know exactly what—suddenly overflowed their banks. "You're a phony," Silas yelled. "Acting like everything is beneath you. You ain't a trainer and you ain't much of a rider and you sure as shit ain't no cowboy. So what are you, Frank?"

Frank set the hat back on his head and lit a cigarette, said, "I know what I am."

"What?"

"And I know what you are. You're nothing but a goddamn sponge."

"Frank," Lena said.

"Sponge," he said again. Spat the word. "And you know it."

And that was the way the night ended: Silas slamming the door and stumbling down the wooden steps to the street and his truck. Lena saying, "Goddamn it, Frank." Frank saying, "Fuck it. Let 'im go." Silas's truck laying black trails off the curb.

The brothers didn't talk to each other for a week. It took that long for them to cool off, to prove to themselves that they hadn't given in to the other, for the fight to be forgotten just enough to let the realities of running a business take precedence. Lena didn't witness the first post-tussle communication. She just saw the two of them discussing something in the middle of the outdoor arena one morning. Like nothing had happened. She wondered for a moment if anything had. In the days between, she'd been a knot of nerves. In the nights she'd slept fitfully. She was happy to see the two of them together, speaking. And she certainly didn't want the fights or silences to continue. But at the same time, she felt a welling of anger: What had it been for? The stress. The long, dark hours of those nights. No, she didn't want strife, but she would have liked to see something result from the anxiety. Were things simply *fine* again?

They spent Thanksgivings in their tiny house and Christmases back at the old place at the stable. And in between the drunken nights and holiday meals, they rode and trained and taught. It was in these years that the boys' father died of lung cancer. Slowly. Painfully. He made it around for a while, still a regular fixture at the arena to watch shows and lessons. He watched the transformation of his barn with silent gravity, never uttering a disparaging word about the boys or their plans, even at the start when they lost his boarders and had to take on loans to keep the outfit afloat. He listened carefully to his sons as they schemed and boasted.

As his life leached away, soaking into his bed and sheets and blankets, as the few breaths he had left escaped his lungs one by one, the boys saw him less and less. Lena watched Frank's eyes avoid his father in bed. Silas Sr.'s mind struggled to keep up with the demands of conversations, Lena could see this — words and memories turning to smoke, impossible to grasp. And as the old man's faculties slipped, Frank's pronouncements of business trivialities grew louder, as if volume could chase away the death lurking between the molecules of air.

"You'll keep them together, I know that much," Silas Sr. said to Lena one time. He was in bed by then, unable to get up even to empty his guts. Lena became familiar with a bedpan and all the functions that necessitated one. Her husband and his brother were a couple hundred yards away giving lessons to the stable's more advanced riders. Or they were negotiating a sale or purchase. Or giving a tour of the facilities to some moneyed parents looking for a place suitable for their precious one's hobby.

The eldest Van Loy took her hand in his, said, "Christ, things fall apart without a woman."

A week later, at a restaurant in San Anselmo, Sandra worried aloud. "I don't know," she said.

"You don't know what, Mum?"

"This isn't exactly the life I would have planned out for you, taking care of the dying patriarch of someone else's family."

"He's my husband's father. It's not like he's a stranger. And that is not my full-time occupation. I'm teaching too."

"The kiddies. Sweetheart, you're too good for that. They're the scraps."

"Thankfully for my students, I don't think of them as scraps."

"But that is what they are, dear. You see that. Lovely and perhaps even somewhat talented scraps, but scraps all the same. Frank assigns the students, yes?"

"I don't have the background he and Silas have."

"Background doing what? You must see that so much of what they do is performance."

"Now he's, what, a charlatan?"

"Not at all. Frank and his brother seem to be enormously gifted. But so are a hundred other people in this county. Like you, for instance. But they have the cowboy hats and the belt buckles and the boots. They get drunk and fight. That is their performance. And the fact is that they are men. You need to be careful about how your life is determined, and by whom."

Lena threw back the last bit of white wine in her glass and poured more from the bottle between her and her mother.

"Now don't be dramatic," Sandra said.

"He's dying. He's just dying and no one else will be there with him."

That night, Lena said to Frank, "He's going soon."

They were in their bedroom. It was summer and the windows

were open, but the air was unrelentingly still. Frank was in his boxers, standing and drinking down a glass of water. He finished and said, "He's been 'going soon' for a long time."

"He's going for real now. Do you understand that?"

Frank glared at her, then let his expression soften.

She said, "You need to understand that."

"I do," he said. He sat on the bed. "Or maybe I don't. I think about death and it's like my mind goes blank. Like an engine overheating or something. It just shuts down. Seeing him, I can feel my brain running hot. Surprised you can't see smoke coming from my ears. Like a cartoon. And then I say to myself, *He's going to be dead,* and the word means nothing to me. I guess this is what religion is for. But you know those particular pants never fit me."

Lena said, "What can I do to help?"

"Woman, you're doing more than your share. I'll get it together. I got it."

But what happened was the exact opposite. Frank's visits became more infrequent. First he missed a day on the pretense of a full teaching schedule and an obligation to look at a horse in Petaluma. Then it would be two days without his heading to the old house. And each time he did come into the old man's room, Lena heard more blathering about day-to-day barn business and more excuses for a quick return to the ease of life outside.

It wasn't until weeks later that Frank was there to witness his father in the full bloom of his disease. It wasn't the violent physical battle that Silas Sr. had been entrenched in a month before, when he was still in the midst of a short-lived attempt at chemo, when the treatments had the old man's body spasming and expelling all manner of waste without warning. Then, the stench of shit and vomit and sweat and death was everywhere. Lena couldn't get rid of the flies and had to hang fly strips to trap them. The doctors quickly recommended abandoning the chemo regimen. No point. He was too far gone. So the night Frank finally returned, it was relatively quiet. Silas Sr. was grimly gaunt, but he didn't flail and moan in agony as much anymore. Lena saw the relief relax her husband's shoulders and soften his face. *This isn't so bad,* his expression seemed to say. And it wasn't. Not compared to the weeks prior. But what Frank didn't understand, despite Lena's trying and trying to explain, was that they'd entered something new. The old man was really and truly approaching death. He would stare at the ceiling for an hour or more. Lena could leave his room to get some dishes done or take care of some stable business that couldn't be put off, and she'd return to find him utterly unchanged. On a few occasions Lena thought he'd already gone. But no. Parts of him were still there in San Geronimo, though it seemed that some aspect of the man was already elsewhere, in the light, the void, the whatever it was.

"Hey, Pop," Frank said.

The old man's eyes broke slowly from their position and made their way to Frank's tall, lean frame.

"How're you doing today," Frank said.

Silas Sr. breathed twice, slowly, and said, "All right."

"Good. That's good. You need anything?" Silas Sr. looked at Frank but did not respond. "Some good things happening out there, Pop. You wouldn't believe the business we're doing. You know we've got three Arabians in the barn right now. Can you believe that? Did you ever think we'd have that kind of horse in those stalls out there?"

Silas Sr. watched his son with an inscrutable, vacant expression until finally, with visible effort, he turned his head. "Lena," he said in a croupy whisper. "Who is that?"

Frank didn't come up to his father's room again, and Lena didn't press him to. Not until two weeks later when Lena recognized something different in Silas Sr.'s breathing, some new level of desperation, and knew that death's final advance was under way. She ran downstairs, hailed a passing boarder — a young girl she'd met only briefly — and told her to fetch Frank and Silas at once. The boys made it and the doctor was called and they were all there and helpless to stop what was happening. It was a Tuesday afternoon in the early fall. The weather had just broken and outside the few people there that day walked their horses across the stable grounds with their chins up high, as if after the summer's hot spell, they were finally able to breathe again.

SEVEN

S ILAS woke the next morning to the sound of a kettle whistle. He watched in silence as Henry crept in from the bathroom and made a press pot of coffee. Silas's head throbbed and he twisted to reach into his bag and retrieve three Tylenol. "You're awake," Henry said. Without water, Silas chewed the pills and swallowed. "You strike me as a coffee man," Henry said. "But I have tea too."

"Coffee," Silas said.

"The girls offered to make breakfast up at the house, if you're interested. To be honest, we don't get too many people out here, so I think they're eager to have a visit."

"Shower?" Silas said.

"If you don't mind me saying, I was hoping you'd ask."

Henry offered to run Silas's things through the wash and said he'd loan him clothes for the time being. The men were about the same size. After showering and drying off, Silas dressed in a white T-shirt and white button-down, a decent pair of wool socks, and his own jeans, no shorts beneath. Henry said the women wanted them at nine o'clock, which gave them a half hour.

They went out to the barn and Disco whinnied at Silas's presence. Henry fetched a flake of hay and tossed it to the mare.

"Been a long time since she had to wait this late for breakfast," Silas said. He stroked her neck and felt her immense muscles working as she chewed. "Sorry, girl," he said.

He could see the stiffness in her steps. She'd been riding long and hard for a couple days now. He bent his creaking knees and rubbed her legs, these magnificent muscles like fingers of lava. He found a brush woven with long, coarse oak and tawny hairs. "Mind?" he said to Henry, who shrugged approval. Silas pulled out as much of the llama hair as he could and used the brush on Disco's muddied belly and legs. He picked the mud and manure from her hooves. There was a bucket hanging from a nail in the wood beam, and Silas poured the rest of his stash of grain into it, then retrieved an apple from the saddlebag and his wood-handled knife from his pocket and cut the apple into eighths and dropped the pieces in. Disco stomped a foot in anticipation. "Don't suppose you've got any molasses," he said to Henry.

"Probably do somewhere." Henry disappeared into the light of outside, returned three minutes later with a jar, the label obscured by the tarry sweetness. Silas struggled mightily with the stuck top and respected Henry for not saying a thing. When he got it open, the black suspension crawled out and down into the pail, grabbing the oats and grain pellets and even the hunks of apple as it rolled over itself to the lowest regions of the bucket's topography. Silas mixed the mess with his hand, Disco snorting, and then let the horse lick his palm and digits clean before allowing her to take the sweet grain in a matter of just a few flops of her lips. Silas ran a hand over the star on her forehead, watching her negotiate the last of the food within the cave of her mouth.

Then to Henry: "I should take her out for a stretch."

"A ride?"

"No, not yet," Silas said. "Just something to keep the kinks out."

"How do you think she'd do with the llamas? Big pasture, plenty of room to roam. Unless you think she'd kick at them or something."

"What's their disposition?"

"Laid back, basically," Henry said.

Silas grinned at the notion of his beautiful horse out mingling with these odd beasts. "No, she won't likely kick." He turned to Disco. "You want to make some new friends?"

At the pasture fence, the men drank their steaming coffee while Silas's mare side-eyed a trio of llamas as they approached and sniffed her.

"Easy now," Silas said.

After a few minutes, they left Disco alone with the llamas and strode up to the main house, where Silas met Maggie's wife, Mira, a lovely and bird-small woman. Maggie wasn't large by any reasonable standard, but with her hips and considerable breasts, she seemed positively huge next to her wife. Mira extended a tiny hand, said, "So nice to meet you." She spoke with an accent that bespoke a global existence.

"Likewise," Silas said.

The house was bright and appointed with dangling green plants on just about every flat surface. Amid these was a long oak table and chairs. The women had put out a spread: coffee and orange juice, croissants with jams, scrambled eggs, bacon, fresh fruit cut into slices. "Christ, I haven't eaten so well in years," Silas said, and he honestly couldn't conjure a memory to dispute this.

They ate and talked most of the time about horses and llamas, each species' habits and needs. The women and Henry discussed shearing; Silas talked jumping and dressage. It was all so pleasant that Silas nearly forgot what had brought him there in the first place, that he was wanted, that he'd killed his brother, that he had no design to speak of save for moving, moving, moving in a vaguely northern direction. Until? He pushed it from his mind and downed a glass of orange juice, practically feeling the vitamins deploying themselves through his body.

"Come back in the spring and you can help us shear," Maggie said.

"Yes," Mira said. "It takes only about six weeks."

"Is that right," Silas said.

"It's a whole operation," Henry said.

"I'd like to see that," Silas said.

After breakfast they went down to watch the horse and the llamas. Disco seemed used to the other animals now, pointedly ignoring them as a kid might younger siblings. The women oohed and aahed when one llama rubbed its body against Disco's belly. Disco half trotted away, came to the fence line, where Maggie and Mira stroked her face and neck.

"Hanoverian," Silas told them. "Maybe my favorite breed of horse. Strong but still fast. And smart. Goddamn smarter than most people. From Germany originally—the breed, not Disco here. She's a California girl."

Mira said, "I used to ride some. I was a girl near Bangalore, but my family moved to the UK when I was ten. I took lessons there, not that I ever got very good."

"My sister-in-law's family is from England," Silas said.

"What part?"

"North. Liverpool."

"Ah," Mira said. "We were southern. Not far from London."

"It's a hell of a life, isn't it?" Silas said. "You start off in India, go to England, and now you're in California shearing llamas. Who could have predicted that?"

"No one," Mira said and smiled.

"What was your path?" Maggie said.

"Me, I was born in a barn and never left."

"No plans to, I suppose," Henry said.

Silas was overcome with pangs of homesickness. He knew with a new depth of understanding that he would never see his stable again. "Oh," he said. "I guess I'll keep riding for a while longer."

The women said they had things to do around the house, projects, said goodbye to Silas, said they hoped to see him again, and excused themselves. Silas watched them ascend the hill and disappear around the corner of their house. Silas and Henry spent another half hour talking and filling up on coffee, and when conversation ran out Silas said, "I'd best be getting out of your hair."

He brought Disco back into the barn and tacked her up. Henry had washed and dried and folded Silas's clothes. Silas thanked him and slipped the still-warm fabric into the saddlebags. He removed the white button-down and untucked the T-shirt, but Henry said, "Keep them. The socks too." Silas nodded a thank-you and shook the man's hand. He buckled the saddlebags and winched the girth one more notch.

"Good-looking horse," Henry said. "I'm glad to have met her."

Silas left Henry there and led Disco up the incline to the house, where he wanted to thank the women for their kindness, and tossed the reins over the porch banister. He knocked on the screen door, waited a moment, went inside. The front room was empty and the table where they'd eaten half cleared. In the next room he found Maggie standing on the other side of the kitchen island, a newspaper spread out in front of her. She looked up at him in alarm, then fear. He didn't need to see his own face staring out in black-and-white, but there he was. Motes of dust twisted in ribbons of window light. Neither Silas nor Maggie breathed.

"You call the cops yet?" he said finally, and then he spotted the phone clear across the room on the counter. He said, "There's a lot more to it than whatever it says in that paper."

"You need to leave," Maggie said, voice tremulous.

"A whole lot more."

"Leave now."

"He really was a son of a bitch. I knew the guy my whole life. He was a son of a bitch if there ever was one."

"Go away now." He could see she was on the verge of a breakdown.

"Yeah, I'm going." But he didn't make a move. And he was suddenly overcome with anger at the woman. It was an anger that, even in the moment, he knew he couldn't justify, and yet there it was radiating from some hard and ugly spot in the core of him. He was desperate, scared, and when he left to go wherever he was going, she would still be here, she and Mira and Henry, all of them comfortable and safe. But now, right there in that bright kitchen, he felt his own power in her trembling voice. It was something. Something he had.

"Is this what it's come to?" he said. "A couple of lesbians living out here, their faggoty husband sleeping down in an outhouse. All of you trying to make a living off these ridiculous, stupid animals.

This is America now?" He didn't mean any of it and hated himself for it even as the words sliced past his teeth. He sounded like some mean and ignorant redneck, the kind of person he would normally disdain, the kind of person he'd always feared he really was. But at the same time, it felt like a great relief. A release. Simple, intoxicating anger against a simple, vulnerable target.

"Please," Maggie said, her voice now barely there.

"Horses. Now there's an animal worth the goddamn time."

Silas took the cord of the phone and yanked it out of the wall and let it drop from his hand to the floor. The screen door banged shut behind him as he bounded down the porch steps.

He mounted his steed and they moved out of the shadow of the house and Silas looked back and saw Maggie and Mira peering down from an upstairs window, a cell phone in Mira's hand. He kicked at Disco's flanks and they moved fast and hard away from the house, back over a rise and into the valley where he'd met Henry the morning before, Disco's hooves crushing and ripping the ground below. They jumped a cedar fence and took a fire road a quarter mile or so before breaking off across another meadow. But on the other side of the wind roaring across his ears, Silas could hear the faint cry of sirens. He pressed harder into the soft of Disco's belly, and the horse put an extra hustle into her gallop. They jumped another fence and moved across a vast field, jumped again, dashed around the side of a humpback hill, and Silas saw a mile down the start of the redwoods. The horse was giving everything she had, and Silas's heart pounded as he slapped and slapped at the old girl's rump. He was up in the stirrups, hunched over. Disco took a particularly ambitious stride, and the back of her head smacked into Silas's nose. Pain shot through his face and deep into his skull. His vision swam and he nearly toppled backward off his mount, but he regained his footing in the stirrups. Moments later he tasted the salt of blood and snot. Still they ran on. And still he heard the sirens, but from which direction Silas could not tell for sure. They became louder. Silas was banking on the cars, wherever they were, whatever they were, not making it over the treacherous terrain. No guarantees, though, and as fast as this horse was, she would soon need to slow.

They made it to the other side of the meadow and entered the dark of the great forest and Silas could feel the sweat that had slicked his back and arms go cold.

EIGHT

THE cartilage that held Frank and Silas together wore away gradually, but that didn't mean that there wasn't a moment when it finally snapped apart for good. Lena was there, and though she'd been witness and occasional party to their disagreements and tussles, she recognized the event as a watershed.

The day started early, at dawn. It was late October and fog rested on the surrounding hills like a whisper. Lena and Frank rolled up to the stable to find Silas already in the barn, his quarter horse Ace tied in the aisle. Silas himself was in his show breeches and boots, a crisp white shirt fastened at the top by a stock pin, though this was obscured for the moment by the dirt-and-manure-stained Carhartt he wore over it all. Lena and Frank, likewise gussied up, coaxed their sleepy-headed horses from their stalls, haltered and tied them, slid the blankets from their backs, and went to work with brushes and curry combs. Lena's horse, a sweet palomino called Luckygirl on account of her touch-and-go breach birth four years before, dropped her head low while Lena picked her hooves.

Silas was just finishing braiding Ace's mane, speaking softly to the gelding as he did. "There you go," he said. "Handsome boy." Lena was used to hearing these quiet conversations. Silas seemed to be in an ongoing dialogue with the horse species. She doubted he even realized he spoke aloud. As stubborn and wild as he could be, he was soft when it came to the horses they kept. Soft in a way that often irritated Frank but that Lena always found surprising and sweet.

When he was done with Ace, Silas brewed a pot of coffee. Frank ambled back to the car and retrieved a coffeecake they'd bought the night before. He cut it into wedges and ate a piece in two bites. Aside from Silas's whispered coos, none of the three humans said a word for a good half hour. When the horses were ready, Lena and Frank and Silas led them to the trailer, hitched up earlier, and then the three of them donned their red coats. It was the first fox hunt of the year.

They drove to Nicasio, to the stable that within eighteen months would be Silas's, and unloaded their horses. Others were already there, nearly all in red coats and stark white shirts and black helmets, nearly all drinking from thermoses of coffee or from glasses of the bloody marys being mixed in the back of a GMC pickup, and chattering about last year's hunts. They weren't real hunts, of course. No actual foxes involved. But the scent had been laid in the hours prior, and they all hoped the trail would be long and a bit tricky, with good lengthy gaps between to challenge the hounds leading the way. On the far side of the meadow, where the huntsmen and huntswomen had stashed their trailers and now stood holding their horses' reins, the priest arrived, a black knit cap atop his head and white cassock dragging in the tall, brown grasses.

Frank and Silas each downed a drink and got another. A

man came around with a tray on which stood delicate glasses of port, and each of the boys took two. Since their father had passed nearly two years before, the brothers had taken to the bottle more often and more seriously, with what looked to be less enjoyment. More than she would have liked, Lena went to bed hours before Frank and in the morning would find their supply of whiskey and beer significantly diminished. God knew what Silas was up to back at the old Van Loy homestead, alone. It was when they were together, though, whether in a period of peace or war, that they drank with such abandon. They could be in a terrible row, arguing over bills or schedules or plans for the business, but neither would return from the kitchen or the bar without a drink for the other. Lena didn't fault them—grief did things to a person—but it scared her each time she saw them passing the point of casual inebriation. Such fuel for such fire.

When everyone seemed sated, the hounds were released from their own trailer and gathered within a circle formed by riders and horses and spectators.

"It is said," the priest began, pulling the cap from his head, "that Saint Hubert saw the sign of Christ while on a hunt. The cross was illuminated within the points of a buck's horns, and he was converted. This is why he is the patron saint of the hunt, and why we invoke his good name on occasions such as this. This morning these are my parishioners." He motioned to the pack rolling and playing and scuffling at his feet. "And I can think of no finer congregation. So we pray that the Lord keeps them safe and free of harm. We pray that they lead the masters true and keep them safe and free of harm. And while we're at it, we pray for the fox, in spirit and absentia. May she be fleet-footed and as clever as her kind is known for. This is the blessing of the hounds, and may they be blessed indeed." He took in hand the aspergillum and shook the holy water onto the pack.

Frank clanked his glass against Lena's. "To the hounds," he said.

"To the hounds," Lena said.

Silas reached in. "The hounds."

"Now," the priest continued, "if the riders will approach." And all of them, red- and black-coated, created a formless mass like a checkerboard gone to chaos, and all removed their helmets and smoothed their hair and knelt before the priest, who hung around each neck a medallion of Saint Hubert. After he'd garnished every rider, he said, "A good hunt to you, and a good day, and I'll see you at the bar." Which got a generous chuckle and a hearty cheer.

The huntsman sounded the horn and the ride began with a leisurely trot. Conversation and laughs. Lena and Frank and Silas knew nearly every one of the others from shows or their own barn stalls, and a good number of them made their way up near the front where the threesome rode and came alongside and bade good mornings. At this point the Van Loy brothers—of which Lena was practically one, as far as most of the other riders there were concerned—had established themselves among the leading trainers in the region, maybe the state. Their students didn't just go to shows; they went to nationals. One had made alternate on the Olympic squad. Theirs was no bullshit boot camp, and if a person was serious and driven and had a modicum of talent, they could mold that individual into something special. "A damn horseman," as the boys might say, even though the vast majority of their boarders and students were women.

They crossed the creek and made the rise on the far side, the hounds leading the way, barking their music, frantic but focused fully on the scent. On the descent, they ran and the riders pressed their mounts to cantering and the cold, wet morning air slicked their skin. The hilltoppers cut long ways, while Lena and Frank and Silas and the rest of the jumpers went straight at the fences and hedges and walls, their horses leaping over, the whole pack of them, led by the hounds and the field master, moving like a wave. Lena's body buzzed with caffeine and vodka and the thrill of the ride. For Lena, this was the high point of the year. This was Christmas two months early. Sweat dripped down her neck and chilled in the dewy wind. Luckygirl relished the sprint and the commotions and rode smoothly across the ecru fields. Though Lena had lived in this area nearly her whole life, it could still feel strange and beautiful, especially on mornings like this when the fog settled in from the coast and the air was filled with the pounding of hooves.

It took just over two hours to follow the scent to its end. The riders cheered as the hounds circled and yelped furiously at the drag, tracked and found hanging from the branches of a wide, vulture-like oak. The hunt hushed briefly as the huntsman issued the mournful "gone home" from his bugle. But the quiet did not last. Chatter and laughs took to the air. Lena and her boys started back with the group at a mild pace, until Lena stole one more look around at the open fields—how often did she ride outside the arena, in *nature?*—and said, "Man, fuck this," and broke off across the meadows at the full gallop. Frank and Silas followed —Lena heard them behind her. She knew the rest of the riders were watching, smiling and shaking their heads at those darn Van Loy boys, no taming them, even though she, Lena, for once led the pack.

They rode up Indian Hill Road and finally cut west and Lena took them all the way to the coast. Their horses lurched into the silky, hot sand of the dunes. The white and gray water burst against the land, and the sun flashed from behind a bank of coastal clouds. Frank said, "Damn right," and leaped from his ride, landed in the sand with a muffled impact. He absently handed his reins to Lena and marched forward to the water, fell backward onto his ass, and tugged off his boots. Britches pulled up just north of his knees, he waded into the froth. Lena and Silas smirked and watched, leaning forward onto the pommels of their saddles. Lena luxuriated in the bracing salt breeze off the water. Frank yelled "Goddamn!" and his wife smiled widely and his brother nodded.

Silas said, "You ever think that we're farther west than the west?" Lena looked at him. He chewed at his bottom lip as if working out nerves, and it only then occurred to Lena that he might be anxious being alone with her. Frank was always right there keeping an eye on everything. But now, though they watched the elder brother there staring down at the water lapping at his ankles, they experienced an awkward intimacy.

"Run that by me again?"

"Like, there's the west, and then past all that there's California. Or at least Marin."

Lena said nothing, but she thought she might've understood him.

He went on, "I've had people say I should be somewhere else. Wyoming or Colorado. Real cowboy country. But I can't imagine being away from this."

"The coast? I didn't know you felt any way about it."

"Shoo," Silas said. "This place is it for me. You can dump

my ashes here at high tide when I'm gone. Better yet, someplace north of here, out in the wild. Some little cove. Shake me out of whatever can you all got me in and let me get eaten up by the fish a bit at a time. You'll do that for me?"

"Me?"

"You. Frank. I ain't likely to have anyone else willing."

"Poor Silas."

"Yeah," he said. "Poor me." He watched the water and his brother dance in it. "I come out here by myself and just look out there," he said. "Just sit here for a while."

"By yourself, huh."

Silas grinned into the wind. "Sometimes I bring a friend."

"Your stable of ladies."

"I don't know about that."

"I can just see it, some young thing coming out here with you not knowing that she's about to fall victim to the Van Loy cowboy charm."

"That what happened with you and Frank?"

She said, "Something like that, I suppose."

Silas said, "Woman, nobody's gonna buy you as a victim."

A gull flew low to the ground, fighting a gust of wind, nearly stationary.

Lena said, "Maybe you should learn to surf. Grow your hair long."

"I can't imagine having time for anything like that. Anyhow, you only get to be good at one thing in this life."

Frank turned to check on his wife and brother, then started back toward them.

Lena said to Silas, "Do you need to be good at something to enjoy it?"

Silas laughed. "How the hell would I know? I've only ever done but one thing."

Frank got to them, boots in hand, his feet socked with sand. He sat down and began slapping at his toes, cleaning them off. "Jesus," he said. "Water that cold, you shouldn't be allowed to call it a beach." He stood and took his horse's reins from Lena's hand. "Well, I could use a drink. How about you, wife, can I buy you a drink?"

They got to the bar an hour later and tied their mounts, alongside a dozen others, to the sawhorses set up outside. Inside, they joined the rest of the riders, who'd already been there for a round or three. Silas shimmied to the bar first and brought back three whiskeys. After the next round, Lena could see which way the day was going. She left the bar—not even knowing if her husband noticed, so caught up was he in the tossing back of whiskey and the recounting of the hunt and the networking and angling for new students and boarders—and rode her horse to the trailer, drove the trailer to where the boys' horses were tied outside the saloon, and brought the whole lot back to the Van Loy stable.

By the time she returned to the bar, the boys were well pickled. Lena would remember that someone had loaded the juke with Fleetwood Mac and that her entrance was soundtracked by the contradiction of "Don't stop thinking about tomorrow" and "What makes you think you're the one who can live without dying?" Frank and Silas were holding court, surrounded by familiar faces, people laughing and nodding and occasionally interjecting but mostly listening to the boys tell their stories, rapt, or at least pretending to be, in due deference to the young men who had, through force of will and innate talent with creatures of the equine persuasion, gained entrée to that world to which they'd not been naturally born. Lena took her place with them. Frank put his arm around her. The others nodded at her. Frank raised a glass and said, "To the hounds!" and the revelers encircling them lifted their own and echoed the pronouncement. Lena pulled Frank's face down to hers and, there in the midst of all the names of the Marin County horse world, planted a kiss on his lips that would flip the pennies from a dead man's lids. Minutes later they were in the john of that dusty bar doing what it was their God-given right to do, being the upstanding married people they were.

By dusk most of the riders were gone, and Frank and Silas and Lena had shed their red coats. They'd staked their claim at the bar. Lena and Frank sat while Silas stood, still bobbing with excitement and weaving with drink. He was recalling all the horses he'd had, the way some men recounted their sexual conquests. These were the ones he'd tamed and trained, the ones he'd loved.

"Ace is up there," he said of the horse he'd been riding that day. A fine, strong bay with four socks and bright, alert eyes. "He's a hell of a horse. I can put any of my students on him, any of them, and they'll learn more from him in one ride than they would from most horses in ten. There's some horses you get on and it's a one-way conversation. You tell 'em what to do and they do it or they don't. But that Ace, boy, he'll talk back. You get it with him, that it's a partnership. No fucking around, he's one of the best I've ridden ever." He leaned in to Lena and held up one finger as if to indicate a special point. "Ever. And I've ridden some goddamn horses."

"Good," Frank said, staring down into his glass of Tullamore Dew.

"Better than good," Silas said.

"No, I mean it's good he's good. Means I made a square deal with Hoskins."

"What deal?"

"Ace," Frank said. "I sold him to Sam Hoskins yesterday. Got twelve grand for him."

Silas stared at his brother with a mix of astonishment and hurt. "The fuck you say."

"Good deal on both sides, brother," Frank said.

"Frank," Lena said. She hadn't known about this sale. If she had, she would have argued against it. This night wasn't the first time she'd heard Silas speak highly of Ace.

"That's my horse," Silas said.

"That's the stable's horse."

"I ride that horse, Frank," Silas said, anger rising. "You know this. I broke that fucker."

"For the stable. For the business. These aren't pets, Silas."

"Christ, Frank," Lena said just before Silas's first punch slammed into Frank's jaw. Lena's husband fell, knocking into the man next to him, falling farther, getting tangled in the legs of the stool.

Silas's boot got Frank once in the gut, but the second kick was intercepted by the stool legs and Frank got a hold and used Silas's leg as leverage to get up and he sent Silas backward into a table of three women, one of whom hit the deck, a full glass of chardonnay across her blouse. And from there it got bad. Frank tagged his brother twice in the ribs before Silas recovered the upper hand, straddled his brother's torso, and laid fist after fist into his face and head and shoulders. All the while cursing him in every fashion one could imagine. People screamed. The bartender was on the phone. Frank managed to get out from under Silas and issue two sickening blows to his face before a posse of men took hold of the two of them from behind, pulled them apart. Both men were wet with blood and saliva and sweat. Both chests heaved with hatred. They fought against the men holding them, but as tough as the boys were, they couldn't shrug off four men apiece. The police were there in no time. Cuffed the both of them. Asked a few questions of the other patrons. Hauled the boys off in separate cars.

Lena, dazed and now suddenly alone, tipped back onto her stool. The people who'd been leveled by the boys' brawl were tended to. The woman cried and pulled her doused shirt away from her chest, and her friends led her to the restroom. A man massaged his ankle. The ones who'd held the boys apart remained in a cluster, not yet ready to break their new bond. Everyone in the bar — or at least it seemed to Lena at the time — took turns watching her. After a moment, a woman came over.

"Are you with those men?" the woman said.

"Yes," Lena said, hardly looking up. "One is my husband. I need to bail them out, I guess."

"Is that what you want to do?"

"Yes," Lena said. "I need to get them."

"Do you want a ride?"

"I have a car," Lena said, but just then a dizziness took over her head and she had to place a hand on the bar. She stared at the finger of whiskey pooled at the bottom of her glass.

Out front, Lena got into a beige sedan. The woman started it up. She was probably a bit older than Lena, a thin, tidy brunette. Lena did not recognize her from Marin's horse world. She realized then that none of the people she did know back at the bar — and there were more than a handful, perhaps a dozen,

people who not long before had been laughing at the boys' antics
—none of them had come to Lena after Frank and Silas were
hauled off.

"They're just like that with each other," Lena said.

"They're friends?"

"Brothers."

"Oh. God." The woman headed south down Nicasio Valley
Road. "Never with you, though," she said.

"Sorry?"

"He doesn't do that with you? Hitting?"

"Oh. No," Lena said. "No, this is between them." Her mouth
curled into a sad grin as she eyed the faint shine of her boots in the
dark of the car. "It's always about them."

The woman took Lena to a bank where she guessed at how
much bail might be set at for the two of them and to be safe took
out all the money the machine would allow, and then they headed
to the police station. Lena told the woman that she'd get a cab
back and that there was no need for her to inconvenience herself
further. The woman pursed her lips and wished Lena good luck
and drove off. Lena never saw her again. In her own drunkenness
and befuddlement at the situation, Lena would not even remember what the woman looked like—only that she'd been there,
that she'd existed and had given Lena a lift.

At dawn Frank was released to his wife. Silas, however, refused her bail, as well as any visitors. Lena and Frank went home
and Frank slept for thirteen hours. Neither of them saw Silas for
two more days, when he showed up back at the barn to trailer the
horses he felt he had claim to. "Sue me for them" were the only
words he spoke. Frank leaned against a stall door halfway down
the aisle.

"You ain't taking Ace," Frank said. "He's already been paid for."

Silas didn't make a move toward Ace. But a week later, after Silas was gone and Sam Hoskins had taken possession, the horse in question turned up lame with a nasty cracked hoof that took six weeks to fuse. Frank had to give a thousand back as well as cover the vet bills just to keep the man from starting talk of lawyers.

❧

It came over the scanner. Police in pursuit. Suspect on horseback. Both women stopped their steeds in unison, and Rain raised the phone's volume as high as it would go, held it out between them. They listened and heard where the police were heading. Rain typed in the name of the town: Garberville.

"About twenty miles," Rain said.

Lena said, "Jesus."

Rain said, "Close."

Lena nodded.

"You sure you want to go ahead?"

Lena said, "We're not going to catch up to him today."

"Not likely."

"Sure he knows they're onto him. He'll be moving at a fast clip now."

Rain said, "And there's—" She stopped.

"What?"

"The funeral."

The words made Lena want to collapse off her horse and dissolve into the earth. "They'll wait for me. Even if they don't, this is more important." She steadied her breathing. She said, "You've been out here long enough."

"I'm not going back if you're not going back."

"I'm not going back."

"Then that's that."

"This isn't your thing."

Rain said, "You're my people."

"I wish you would go back." Lena looked around her at the smattering of oaks and firs. Her mind went to the coast, where she'd rather have been. She said, "If we get to him, you stay back. You don't get near him. You ride the other way. Promise me."

"Okay."

"Promise me."

"I promise."

Lena took off her helmet, brushed the bangs off her forehead, replaced the helmet, fastened the strap. "Which way?" she said. Rain consulted her phone and pointed northeast.

They broke into canters and didn't talk for two hours, at which point they spotted a roadside sign announcing the entry to the Mendocino National Forest. The trees loomed tall and dense. "We'll skirt it," Lena said, and she led her compatriot north along the western edge of the forest at a trot. The scanner had police focusing a good ten miles farther up. Lena took a swig of water; she didn't have much left. At a creek they stopped and let the horses drink. The women stretched their backs and necks and shook out their legs. Then they rode on, following the creek northward five or so miles until it cut west. They kept north into the wood.

At a two-lane highway they climbed the embankment, and the horses' shoes clanked against the pavement. Lena heard the rush of a car just before a police siren bleated once, twice.

"Fuck," Rain said.

Lena said, "Go," and maneuvered Pepper down the far side

of the embankment, into a denser wood. The siren sounded again and Lena could hear the car cut onto the shoulder just a few dozen feet behind them.

A voice called through a speaker, "You two on the horses, stop." Two doors shut. Other, fainter sirens in the distance. Lena sighed and eased Pepper to a halt. "Okay," she said to herself and to Rain and to their horses and to Frank and to no one.

NINE

UNDER the cover of the deep woods, Silas slowed Disco to a walk. He caught glimpses of the sun through the bower and oriented himself. His heart thumped away as if it might burst. He ducked low branches and panned the woods with his eyes, absent-mindedly stroking Disco's neck all the while. The ground was carpeted in soft needles and softer dirt and was relatively quiet to move across, but each of the horse's footfalls sounded to Silas like an explosion. Sirens wailed in the distance, but they didn't seem to be getting any closer. He reached back and pulled a button-down shirt from his saddlebag and wriggled into it. Tried to steady his breathing. Of course they knew he was heading north by now, so he steered the horse eastward, away from the noise of the sirens and deeper into the forest.

Over the next three hours he ascended the eastern mountain ridges, occasionally happening upon something like a trail, but mostly making his own, weaving through the trees and skirting the denser thicket. Silas dismounted for the steeper inclines and pulled Disco by the reins. His leg muscles throbbed, shaking from effort and the extended dose of adrenaline. He could hear the sirens now only when he tried. On a stretch of flat he stopped, drank from one of the two bottles of water he had. It wasn't enough, not for himself, let alone the horse. He poured the rest into Disco's outstretched lips and the horse lapped it with a desperation that sent a quake of shame through Silas.

They came upon a gravel forest highway, a wide winding road meandering up toward the peaks of the ridge. They'd be more exposed here, but the riding would be far easier. The horse couldn't keep going on that ragged land much longer. Already, each step was an effort. On one side of the road the mountain rose, the specifics of it being lost to a sea of indistinct trees. The other side, where they'd come from, dropped away to the valley. Silas's entire view was of green and brown. No towns, no roads to be seen from his vantage, though he knew the roads were there. The question he faced was whether to continue up the forest highway, away from the cops, or down toward somewhere he might be able to find some provisions. He took stock of what he had: two cans of soup, a bottle of water, a knuckle of bread and an apple from Henry, half a thermos of two-day-old coffee, two bottles of wine. He gave the apple to Disco and drank the old coffee himself.

He had just grasped the saddle to lift himself up when he heard a sound. A buzzing in the distance growing into a small thundering. He cast his eyes upon the valley and for nearly a minute saw nothing. Then, there to the southeast, he spied the helicopter. He took up the reins again and rushed Disco to the far side of the road. Man and horse scrambled over the embankment and into the dark of the woods, up the hill, aiming for whatever patch of trees seemed the densest. Disco struggled and tripped in holes and over roots and fallen branches, and Silas stumbled alongside, but still he pulled the bay onward.

The noise of the helicopter faded, then returned louder, then faded again. It was circling, Silas understood. For minutes it would disappear behind some peak or another, only to reappear closer than it had been before. He had the forest to blanket them. He kept on until, finally, exhausted, he stopped in a particularly dark grove and collapsed to the ground. The horse snorted loudly with each breath, her coat now glistening with sweat.

They stayed there the rest of the day. Silas listened to the helicopter circle and circle again. It didn't get to where they hid, and just before dusk its sound faded for good, but he knew it would be back at dawn and that eventually it would hover over them. In the diminishing light of dusk, he took Disco out into a nearby meadow for grazing, keeping his horse near the edge of the field and keeping his own eyes on the darkening sky. Back beneath the forest canopy, Disco protested against the developing cold, stomping in place, shudders overtaking her withers. Silas fished out one of the T-shirts that Henry had washed and rubbed the horse's back where the saddle had been, trying to soak up some of the sweat. Still the horse snorted. "I know," Silas muttered, wriggling into his coat and hunkering down against a fallen pine, closing his eyes. "I know, goddamn it."

❧

Within a week of the fox hunt Silas was teaching at the outfit in Nicasio. He'd heard about Ace's cracked hoof and the rumor that he'd somehow had something to do with it. To Silas the notion that he would hurt a horse, especially one he felt a kinship to, was absurd. Not so to others, apparently. Students would shyly pass along the latest talk: He'd snuck back to the old barn in the night and did the job there and then. "What did I use, a hammer and chisel?" he would ask, feigning disinterest, busying his eyes and hands with grooming or a piece of tack. The students would not answer. He'd had nothing to do with it, though he knew that Frank believed otherwise.

Most of Silas's students came over from the old barn, and he gained a few more without trying hard at all. He brought with him a considerable reputation. It might have been that some trainers coming to a new barn would have told these curious young riders to stick with their teacher. Professional etiquette. Some might have lied, said they had a full schedule, so as not to disturb the delicately balanced environment they'd just entered. This never occurred to Silas. He couldn't have cared less about the other trainers, even the ones he knew. He approached riders in the barn aisles or perched on the arena fence. Told them he'd been watching them ride (which was often, though not always, the truth) and he could see potential. "Good natural form," he'd say. Or "You've got instincts, no doubt about that." He commended them on possessing the things that could not be taught while remaining conspicuously silent on the training they'd received for the things that could. These riders would then, often after extensive self-admonishment, sheepishly explain to their old trainers that they were interested in trying Silas out. They'd heard such things about him. They owed it to themselves to be open. And that would be that. He even got a few of Frank's old disciples, which pleased him more than anything else could.

He bought an Airstream and paid the barn's owner a fee to park the thing on an unused bit of dirt a hundred or so yards off the stable, the ground beneath his tubular home hard and cracked as a shattered windshield. Nights, he would sit in a low-slung camp chair, drink the wine he was developing a taste for, and watch the shadows of horses and humans move across the barn windows. The hills all around appeared like men hunched in prayer.

Within a few months Silas was the primary draw for the stable. Most of the other trainers had left for other barns or simply resigned themselves to taking on the kids and older folks. Silas got the good ones, the late-teens and twentysomethings, the ones with the potential. He worked them hard, often yelling, sometimes storming out and declaring the lesson a waste of his time. And that was it; this was *his* time. Students were lucky to be sharing in it. He was a tyrant, sure, but an effective one. His students rode better, partly out of fear of incurring his wrath. And as a result, they went to shows and won blue time and time again.

It didn't take long before the owner of the barn approached Silas about buying the place, a proposition Silas deliberated on only in order to drive the price down. It was a sprawling outfit, with open, rolling land for miles on all sides. He wanted it. He knew Frank was a better businessman, but Silas was a better trainer. He was a better rider. And now that they were apart, the distinction would become apparent. Of course, Frank had Lena, whom Silas knew to be a hell of a rider and a hell of a teacher. But Silas counted on Frank fucking that up. She was better than Frank, too, and this Frank would not allow himself to admit. More than anything else, Silas wished his father and mother were still around so that they could see what was about to happen, see Silas prove the lot of them wrong.

He took over the stable and brought in a few young trainers to work under him. He expanded the primary barn and built a secondary one for show housing, but soon that too filled with regular boarders. He dug out the old outdoor arena and laid down a new ring with fresh fencing and a new footing mixture that was both more cushioned and firmer than any surface he'd ever ridden on. He rebuilt the paddocks, widening the area of each, adding a dozen more, and installing automatic watering troughs.

He also introduced dressage to his teaching repertoire. This was something Frank had talked about doing, but he'd never taken the plunge. Silas figured that despite his habit of putting business first, second, and last, his brother still had a fear of this sort of riding. Though it likely would have been profitable, it was a bit too removed from the old saddle-handle-and-braided-bridle ways they'd grown up with, and so the talk remained just that for all those years. But not for Silas, not anymore. This was not to say that he entered into the endeavor with confidence and gusto. On the contrary, he was scared shitless. Posting and jumping were all well and good, but the movements a horse was asked to make in dressage were a whole other undertaking. He'd trained horses to change leads back in his reining days, sure, but that was just the start in dressage. Extensions, counter canters, and half halts. Those things the untrained eye barely registered but that could make or break a ride in a show. And then there were the fireworks, all those piaffe and passage gaits with the horses dancing damn near in place. The things even dopes like Silas could see. He was determined to learn them all, the invisible and the visible. Spent his nights staying up late drinking and reading about the various techniques, then shook off his hangovers at first light before any boarders arrived and took a beautiful palomino called Donovan out to the arena. Donovan had done some of this with a previous owner and reluctantly recalled the movements under

Silas's clumsy guidance. He felt like a fool learning to ride once again, but this here was what old Frank would have called "re-branding." Silas would beat the fucker at his own game.

At the end of his first year he was broke and dependent on every dime of board coming in to cover his bills and loans. But, he thought each evening as he sat outside the Airstream, even if he had no cash, he had the best barn in Marin. He knew it. And, more important, he knew Frank knew it.

This, he supposed, was the reason he was certain it was Frank — probably drunk out of his gourd — who smashed the windows of the Airstream one night. Silas came home from a tasting to find nuggets of glass everywhere. That was how the war was begun in earnest. A childish first strike. And Silas responded soon in kind, sneaking back to the old stable and slicing the tires of Frank's truck and trailer, leaving them both ovaling their rims. Even then Silas knew this was a stupid thing to do. But what else to do? What else when he was bored and lonely and resentful and working his way through a second bottle of cabernet? They went on like this for nearly three years, Silas and his brother trading petty blows aimed at each other's property. A keyed car door. The burgling of a home. More smashed-in windows. Repeat.

Then the gossip and rumors and lies began. It started with the resurfacing of that bullshit about Ace's cracked hoof. People were talking about Silas's treatment of the animals in his care, even though Ace hadn't been in his damn care at that point. Didn't matter. Silas countered with questions about just how effective a trainer Frank was, how much he'd depended on his younger brother. Then came talk of Silas's relationships with his students — some of whom had indeed retired with him to the Airstream on occasion. They stole students and boarders. And rumors spread of Frank's use of tranks at shows. Silas imagined that might have lost his brother a student or two, maybe more, which was just the point.

Colic ran through Silas's place one especially chilly March morning. It had started simply enough, a couple horses stubbornly refusing to exit their stalls, the owners pulling on their halters, grunting and laughing.

"Something in the air this morning," one said.

"Come on, lazybones," said the other.

Silas was roosted atop his barstool at the door of the barn, going over his bills for the month—he was a shit bookkeeper and in a near-constant simmering panic about forgotten numbers and missed payments—and not really listening to the conversation. It was the background noise of the place: people trying to coax horses from there to here, dancing between loving coos and halfhearted reprimands. It was only when a student of Silas's—a young woman he'd slept with back in the Airstream a handful of times—came into the barn and said, "Something's wrong," that he knew this morning was different. Fear alit on that freckled face he'd come to enjoy so. He followed her to the paddock where her Paint mare was on the ground, breathing heavily. "She won't get up," the woman said. She put a hand on Silas's arm. Then again: "Something's wrong."

"Goddamn," he breathed. Opened the gate and strode to the woman's horse, knelt down and stroked the mare's neck. Her wide, panicked eyes rolled to watch him. He set his ear to her ribs and listened to the heightened rolling of her heart. He scanned the paddock and went to a pile of manure. The lumps were old and dry and crumbled in his hand. Nothing fresh. He stood and hopped onto the second railing of the fence and perused the grounds, took in the scene with new eyes. A dun gelding was down three pens over, as was a filly he'd brought in just days before. He found one of his own horses rolling in distress. "Get the feed out of all these pens," he told the woman. "Dump the water. Get her up and walking."

A hundred yards away one of his men was pushing grain to the far paddocks. "*¡Oye,* Manuel!" he called. He got the man's attention, pointed at the wheelbarrow, and cut fingers across his throat. "*¡No mas!*" Across the grounds another worker was divvying up flakes of alfalfa. "Felipe," Silas yelled, running to him, "*no mas* alfalfa."

"*¿Por qué?*"

"No good," he said. "I don't know. Get it all back out, then help walk the horses. Tell Manuel too."

The boarders there were already in their stalls scooping grain out of their horses' buckets and pulling flakes of alfalfa and hay. Then they went in to other stalls to carefully retrieve the feed from horses that weren't theirs, all the while saying "Sorry" and "I know" in sweet tones. Silas called his vet and his feed man. He explained what he was seeing and repeated the symptoms the horses were exhibiting. Vet got there within an hour — good woman, that one — and took vitals on all the horses showing signs of colic. Nine in all. She listened to their bellies.

"Doesn't seem like twisted gut," she said. "But I guess we knew that by the epidemic here." All across the stable grounds, as people were leading horses aimlessly back and forth, they kept an eye on the vet and Silas. The vet performed rectal exams and gave the affected horses analgesics for pain and laxatives to help move their digestive tracts. It took the whole of the morning and into the afternoon. "Keep 'em walking," she said. "And pray for poop."

Silas went to the feed barn and climbed into the loft and snipped the baling wires and ripped through the alfalfa. Soon he found the dark, compacted matter at the center of a bale.

The feed rep showed up midafternoon, stepped out of his truck, and adjusted his company hat. "What have we got?" he asked as Silas approached.

"I'll show you what we got," Silas shouted. He took the rep to where he'd tossed the contaminated bales from the loft. "We got a problem is what we got. We got nearly a dozen horses with their guts full of goddamn mold."

"Now let me see here," the rep said. "Just settle down." He knelt and inspected the alfalfa. "Well, hell," he muttered.

"Mold," Silas said again.

"Yeah," the rep said nearly to himself. "Boy, that's what it looks like, huh."

"What it is."

"How many bales?"

Silas pointed to the three he'd tossed. "These so far. You're about to check the rest of the fifty."

"Use your phone? I got to call my guy. If the issue's back at storage, I need them to know."

"The problem ain't here, bub," Silas said. "We haven't seen a drop of rain since this last delivery. And I had this roof redone half a year ago anyway. This loft ain't the problem."

"Well," the rep said.

"Yeah," Silas said. "Well."

"I'll call my guy."

Silas brought the cordless and the rep called, started explaining the issue to the man on the other end. Then, as he was repeating the details of the situation—a simple situation, as Silas saw it, clear as day—for what seemed like the third time, the rep stopped and said, "Wait a minute here." He was kneeling down in the busted bales, covered in dust and husks head to toe. He pulled the baling wire from under the alfalfa. He pulled out another and another. "Hang on," he said, not quite to Silas, not quite into the phone. Then he said straight to Silas, "This isn't our wire."

Silas looked at him.

"We use the regular galvanized type," the rep said, "not this black." Silas didn't respond, didn't blink. The rep set the phone down and Silas heard the muffled voice in the receiver say, "Mark?" The rep bounded up the ladder to the loft. "See," he said, then: "Watch out, now," and he pushed a bale over the side. "See, that wire? That's ours. Silver. These ones you pulled out have this black annealed kind. It's better wire, to be honest, but it isn't what we use."

"So someone used a different wire," Silas said.

"I've never seen anyone use this at our company."

The rep came down again. Silas tried to steady his heaving breath, said, "What are you suggesting?"

"I'm suggesting that these bales of moldy feed didn't come from us."

By then a handful of Silas's boarders were gathered at the mouth of the feed barn, and they saw Silas curl in his fingers and set that fist hard into the rep's jaw. They saw the rep hit the ground. They heard Silas yell, "Don't you try to fuck me, you shit."

Two boarders stepped up quickly and flanked Silas and cautiously set their trembling hands on his chest. "Silas, don't," one said. The one he'd been sleeping with, the one whose horse first went down, the one whose face he liked so very much, stayed behind, her hand set over her gaping mouth, watching.

By the time the police came, Silas knew it had been Frank. The understanding came like a leavening. One moment Silas raged against the feed rep and the next he felt a curious calm, the sort of calm that comes when the world, at least for a quick moment, makes sense. Son of a bitch poisoned his horses. How he'd done it—how Frank had gotten those moldy bales up in the loft—Silas didn't know, but there was no doubt it was him. Silas almost laughed.

An hour later he was cuffed for popping the feed rep, spent a day in jail, and saw a judge who questioned why a grown man, a business owner, a teacher, for heaven's sake, would act so stupidly. Silas stood in the arraignment room. "Well, my horses were sick and I thought he was trying to fuck me but I see now I was probably wrong about that."

The judge eyed Silas and said, "Yes, well, regardless," and sentenced him to community service wherein he was to spend twenty hours over the next six months telling kids in the rougher areas of San Francisco about the glorious horse life.

TEN

LENA and Frank lived in relative peace for the next decade. In fact, Lena would recall this as the time when their marriage was at its best. The period when it felt like their strides were nearly perfectly matched. With Silas gone they drank less, got more sleep. Made love more often. They vacationed, even occasionally in places that had nothing to do with horses. New York. Rome. Or spent simple, long weekends hoofing the hills of the city and sleeping late. Frank even took an interest in the more elevated reaches of culture, accompanying Lena to museums and galleries, concerts that didn't involve pedal steel guitar.

One night they were invited to the home of one of their wealthiest boarders for a reception for an Italian opera singer touring the States. Frank hesitated only a moment before agreeing to attend. In an opulent living room punctuated by figureless expressionist art, the singer offered a brief aria, a Verdi crowd pleaser, her voice undulating with the smoothness of blown glass and finally reaching a soaring peak that filled the parlor with a sound at once unnatural and utterly elemental. Lena looked up at her husband's face to find it rapt, his mouth ajar ever so slightly. A momentary silence followed the aria's conclusion, and then applause overtook the room, no clapping louder or more rapid than that of Frank's big horseman's hands. He fit two fingers into his mouth and issued an ear-twisting whistle. And then he cupped a hand to the side of his mouth, called "Bravo!" and let loose a hearty roar of laughter, as if no other reaction could suit such a wondrous display of virtuosity. The rest of the crowd broke protocol and joined him, snickering and grinning, and the opera singer smiled shyly and bowed her head Frank's way.

In this moment and others, Lena felt again as she had when they'd first met and then married. Hers was the tall man in the Stetson, the one who could charm with a side smile, a wink, the one who shot her fun, lusty looks across a party room and who danced terribly with a tumbler of whiskey in hand, who knew how to make love to her at night and sometimes in the day and who didn't bother her often in the morning. This was the time, Lena would later think, when Frank became most *Frank*. All aspects of the man — his roughness, his intelligence, his boyishness, his ambition — were in equilibrium. This was the Frank that she hoped people would recall when they thought of him. It was the Frank she wanted to remember.

And yet through all this, the boys' feud continued. Silas broke into their house at least once a year. Stole money and old family photos. Cracked Lena's Springsteen and Emmylou records. Even pissed on their couch, the childish prick. Their son, Riley, came along and grew bigger and knew Silas only as a faint specter hovering around their otherwise mild lives. "He's nobody, sweetheart," she'd say to her boy, pulling him to her, wrapping him up. "Nothing for you to worry about." But she shook at the thought that he would approach Riley one day, outside school perhaps, or while he chalked the sidewalk down from their house. Talk to him, scare him. Even snatch him up. He was a vindictive and unpredictable man, and he hated Frank and, she supposed, herself by connection. It wasn't impossible to imagine him taking her boy.

She was under no illusion that Frank had been sitting out the feud entirely. She knew her husband and she was not in the habit of deceiving herself. But still she could not accept that he'd been as felonious as his brother. Silas, it seemed, had become unhinged. By all accounts he was winning whatever war he thought they were engaged in; since he'd left, money slid away from the old stable in San Geronimo like runoff. Yet he continued.

Silas was a master trash-talker, and that kind of game went far in the gossipy horse world there in Northern California. All those bored, moneyed folks looking for drama to liven up their days. And if you're craving drama and you meet the Van Loy boys, you stop looking and start palavering.

Silas had the whole area thinking he'd been the heart, soul, backbone, and balls of the operation. Which was a joke. Silas was a con man. A decent trainer, sure — Lena would allow that. He was better than most. He knew a horse's mind as well as he knew its body. But despite his repeated claims to the contrary, he was no better than Frank. Lena had seen students bloom and flourish under Frank's tutelage. Silas was good, yes, but he certainly shouldn't have been able to compete with Frank and Lena, who herself had become one of the best respected trainers in the county. The two of them complemented each other. Students might slack for Lena from time to time, but when Frank was around, they double-timed, put an extra bit of air between their asses and the saddles. Likewise, when Frank was too blunt with one, Lena was there to offer an encouraging word. Not that she was a pushover. She might have been soft in comparison to Frank, but students would never have described her as such. In fact, the more experience she accrued, the less patience she had for laziness and excuses. One spring afternoon she was cleaning her bridle in the tack room when Rain, then just seventeen, came in and asked if they might talk. "I feel like I'm not connecting with Dexter," she said. Dexter was a black gelding school horse she'd been riding for a month.

"It takes a while to get used to each other," Lena offered.

"Maybe I could try Penny?"

"Penny has enough riders. Too many, in fact. Anyway, she's no easier than Dex. Harder, probably. She's got a stubborn streak."

"Any of the other ones?"

"It's the summer, Rain. You know how it gets with the camps and the pony clubs."

Rain shuffled her feet. "It's just—it's been really hard."

Lena threw the bridle onto a trunk; the bit clanged against a rivet. "Riding is hard," she said. "And it isn't going to get any easier ever. Certainly not by standing around griping and blaming a perfectly good horse for your frustration."

This was a memory tinged not with guilt at having spoken harshly to the girl, but rather with a sort of pride—pride that on some level, Lena's approach had worked, that Rain stuck with it, learned to be a horsewoman. And this happened over and over, with dozens of students.

So those notions that Silas sent aloft into the horse world's ether, that he'd carried the old Van Loy stables, were nonsense. They were, however, effective. As Silas's operation grew, Frank and Lena's business at the old barn slowed and shrank. They still had their core boarders and students, but attracting more became difficult, and soon half their stalls stood empty. They cut corners and cut back and scraped by for a couple years, Frank all the while scheming to pay back his brother tenfold for sullying their reputation. What they'd built there in San Geronimo before Silas's departure was already too large to maintain, and yet every plan Frank came up with seemed to somehow involve expansion. The Van Loy boys were never short on ego. It wasn't until one day when Frank was outlining a new plan for buying up some of the land on the west edge of the property to develop a steeplechase course that Lena let loose her own ideas.

She said, "What if we went the other way?"

"What other way?"

"Small," she said. They were in their bedroom. It was nearly ten and Riley, then in junior high, was wrapping up his homework in the next room. "What if we sell this off and start up with something else. I'm tired of this competing, Frank. So let's play a different game. We'll have a few stalls, a dozen. We'll focus our energy on teaching. No more big shows. No events. A couple small, good camps in the summer. Low overhead. We go small."

Frank sat on the edge of the bed and let his shoulders slump, taking on the architecture of the resigned. "All right," he said. "We'll start looking. Talk to an agent about putting this place on the market. Let the miserable fucker win."

"It isn't about that."

"It is."

"Why does it have to be?"

Frank was silent a moment, then cleared his throat and said, "Because we're brothers."

But his reluctant acceptance of the new plan soon turned to excitement as they looked at stables up for sale and imagined all they could do with a smaller, more concentrated approach. Frank was the one who'd first used the word *boutique,* to Lena's surprise and barely concealable amusement. And this excitement he developed was the reason it hurt Lena so badly when Frank shot his brother.

He hadn't talked about his brother in months, and without that cloud hanging over them they became what Lena had always wanted them to be: a happy couple working and raising their son and slowly, quietly getting older. They found the new stable in Fairfax, sold the old place, and started anew. So when Frank told her that he wanted to see Silas, she felt her stomach contract.

Frank said, "I think we can settle things."

Lena shook her head. "That is not what will happen."

She wasn't at their bungalow when Silas came over. When it happened. They were still fixing up the new house in Fairfax, and she was there that whole day and evening, painting the bedrooms with Riley — an activity she enjoyed immensely and found therapeutic. As far as she knew, Frank was packing up the kitchen — an activity she abhorred. The phone had already been set up at the new place and she'd talked to Frank just a couple hours before. He said he was making progress and taking a little break. Despite significant slowing, Frank still drank, but it didn't occur to Lena that this might be what he meant by a break.

Should she have felt some change in the air, some charge buzzing in her ears? She didn't believe in such things. *Rubbish,* Sandra would have declared such notions, and Lena would have agreed. But later, thinking back on this day, she would be mildly surprised that she had not sensed a thing. Her life was changing, and yet she remained, for hours, utterly unaware. The sun had slipped down beneath the horizon by the time Lena and Riley completed painting the two main bedrooms. They cleaned up and stopped at a pizza place for takeout, and Lena stood and watched Riley play *Ms. Pac-Man* while they waited for their food. They ate the crusty corners of the pizza in the car on the way back to the bungalow. Riley ran up the front steps of the house. Lena came along slowly. After he'd gotten to the porch and entered, Riley stood in the living room holding the pizza box, his back to his mother.

Lena said, "Sweet?"

"Where's Dad?"

A couch cushion tossed. Tumbler glass on coffee table overturned. The tray of the CD player hanging out like a tongue. Just next to where Lena stood in the open doorway, the white wingback chair was flecked with red. Finally, her eyes found the blood soaked into the rug.

Lena said, "Jesus," then called, "Frank?" She took the pizza from Riley and set it on the coffee table. She told the boy to go back down to the car and lock the doors and wait there.

"Mom, why?" Riley said.

Lena said, "Please."

She crept through the cramped house but found no one. All was as it should have been, except that she discovered the wooden gun box that they kept on a high closet shelf out and open and empty.

She went to the car and drove with Riley to the old stable in San Geronimo. A night fog had settled over it. No one was there. No people, no horses. A ghostly silence.

When they got back to the house, the light on the answering machine blinked. As Frank's voice issued from the tiny speaker,

Lena inhaled as if she hadn't breathed in hours. But the relief was short-lived.

"Yeah, it's me. I'm, uh, in jail. Silas got shot. And I guess . . ." The speaker buzzed as a scratching noise sounded—Frank's beard against the plastic of the phone. Then his voice came back. "I guess I did it. Guess I shot him myself. Don't think he's dead, but who knows. Anyway, come on down here if you want. Don't know when I'll be arraigned. I never shot anybody before, but I imagine it might take a while. I guess maybe the neighbors might watch Riley." He signed off with his customary "All right." And that was it. Lena's husband was in jail. Her brother-in-law might be dead. Lena turned and was surprised to find Riley standing there, tears running down his cheeks. She'd forgotten he was with her.

She said, "Jesus. Sweetie."

Silas lived, of course. He'd been shot in the gut, and the lead passed through him and kept going out the open front door behind him. Cops never found it. The doctors at the emergency room and then farther down into the hospital where he spent the next two weeks had never seen such a clean gunshot wound. Sliced through one of his kidneys, but other than that. They shrugged. Said it was a miracle shot. Damn lucky, they declared Silas.

Frank claimed he was giving the gun—an antique that had belonged to their father—to Silas. A gift. An overture. A gesture of apology and forgiveness. He said he'd invited his brother to the bungalow to make peace, that he'd had enough of the whole goddamn mess they'd made of things and that he hadn't known it was loaded and that the thing just went off. Didn't know how or why. He said he loved his brother, through it all.

When it was his turn to talk, Silas told it differently. In the courtroom ten months later he said he'd been invited over to hash things out, yes, and that he'd come in good faith. Said there hadn't been any accident, that Frank was drunk — as was he — and that they argued and that the elder Van Loy boy held the gun out and shot as purposefully as anybody could.

"What did you argue about?" his lawyer asked him.

"Lot of things."

"Can you give us any specifics?"

"Hat," Silas said. "Old Stetson. See, Frank's business isn't going well and he wanted me back with him to try to save it. His wife's got some silly plan about a new outfit, but Frank said that we could reconcile, get back to where we'd been. Me and him like it used to be."

"And what did you say to this?"

"Said why would I? My business is good. Better than good. Then I thought about it and said, fine, give me the hat and we'll give it a go."

"You were going to rejoin your brother in business?"

"I wanted to see how serious he was. Little test. He's always liked that hat a good deal."

"And then what happened?"

"Then the son of a bitch shot me in the gut. He muttered something like 'Forget it' — I didn't hear him exactly — and he laid me out in the doorway."

Frank's lawyers kept him quiet and offered a procession of experts on guns and trajectory and the like, and together they were able to plant a seed of doubt. The unpredictability of an old gun like that. After seven weeks of trial, Frank plea-bargained down to reckless endangerment. He spent fifteen months in the minimum-security wing of San Quentin, during which time Lena opened the new stable, helped Riley adjust to high school, and visited her husband weekly, never once asking if he had indeed asked his brother to rejoin him in business, if through all their plans together for a fresh start, he'd been playing her for a fool. She didn't want to know. It was a painful bit of pride she would force herself to swallow. She imagined some might chide her for the decision, claiming that the truth was always paramount. Those people could go to hell. She wanted her husband back, her son's father, and if that meant living with the mystery, then so be it.

❧

"Mrs. Van Loy," Detective Ortquist said. "Can you help me understand what you're doing out here?" He was in the driver's seat of a gray Chevy. Lena sat on the passenger side. The car was stationary but running, and the windows were shut, making Lena feel trapped. Which, of course, she was. Ortquist was maybe forty-five, fifty, tops. Had the usual cop sternness, but Lena could tell he was a decent sort underneath. A faint ring of pockmarks edged his jawline, and he wore some kind of cologne, not offensive or obnoxious but pungent enough to make Lena momentarily self-conscious about the aroma she was giving off after days in the saddle.

She said, "Can I open this window?"

"No." Ortquist turned a dial on the dash and cool outside air came through the vents, solving nothing. "What are you doing here?"

Lena breathed in, out. "Riding," she said.

"So it's, what, a coincidence, your being in this particular spot? So close to where we think your brother-in-law might be?"

Lena said nothing. She'd seen Ortquist before, on the day of
Frank's death. He'd been with the other police, the ones who'd
questioned her at her house. But he'd said nothing. She liked him
for knowing how to shut the fuck up when a woman had just lost
her husband.

Through the window she watched Rain standing on the
shoulder of the road holding both horses' reins. Pepper and Major seemed on edge, stepping in place, swinging their rears, and
Rain had to give each of them a quick yank to get them in line.
Three uniformed police stood near, their eyes molesting Rain and
glancing back toward the car where Lena and Ortquist sat.

"You're going after him? Is that it?"

"I don't seem to be going anywhere right now." *Jesus Christ,*
she thought, *he's getting away.*

Ortquist said, "A more paranoid officer of the law might
think there was something else happening."

"Such as?"

"When was the last time you saw or spoke to Silas?"

"For the love of God."

"Tuesday you said it'd been seven years. Or thereabouts. Sure
you aren't forgetting something?"

She nodded. Why she'd lied about this, and why she continued to, she did not fully understand. She'd talked to Silas just
weeks before.

Ortquist said, "We never said anything about finding his
trailer. How'd you know he's on horseback?"

"So you knew all along?"

"We did. How did you?"

Lena sighed. "A friend saw him. Told me. But I would have
figured it out eventually anyway."

"What's your friend's name?"

"Carly."

"Carly Nichols," Ortquist said.

"She called you, then."

"You didn't think to tell your contact at the department?"

Lena said nothing. One of the police outside, the one who'd stopped her and Rain in the first place, lit a cigarette. Lena pressed the window button, but it did nothing. "Open this window, please," she said to Ortquist, and he waited a moment before unlocking the mechanism and then nodding once. She lowered the window and leaned out. "Do not smoke near those horses, sir," she called out. She pointed. "Put that out. Those animals don't need to breathe in that poison." The cop hesitated, then stepped into the road, took one last drag, and stomped the butt out into the concrete.

Ortquist said, "Your son has been out looking for you. Half out of his mind with worry."

Lena continued to watch the cop outside. She said to Ortquist, "What is that idiot thinking? Never mind the animals—there's been something of a drought in these parts going on thirty years."

"Mrs. Van Loy."

"Best and brightest, huh."

"I could bring you in for interfering with an investigation. Do you understand that? It would be for your own good."

"We haven't interfered with a thing. You wouldn't even know I was here if that moron hadn't happened upon us."

Ortquist said, "Tell me about the girl."

"Rain."

"Tell me about her."

"She works for us."

"How'd she end up out here with you?"

"She needed a long ride. Someone she knew well was murdered."

Ortquist watched Lena. She didn't look at him but she could tell. The way he breathed, she could hear him looking.

She said, "I told her to stay back."

Ortquist said, "Excuse me, but this is a big pile of shit, and you know it. You being out here. This is a big fucking mess for me."

"I imagine it would be."

He consulted documents in a manila folder and on a tablet. Without looking up, he said, "Let's talk about the horses that died a few years back. Four of them, is that right?"

"What is there to talk about?"

"You tell me."

"Silas killed them."

The incident had almost done their business in, snuffed it out completely. It had taken five years, but they'd finally gotten past the whispers of the shooting, which had been nearly constant until then. Lena took a more central role in the training and acted as the public liaison for the operation, and with Frank in the background, they healed their bruised reputation and filled the fifteen stalls of the new stable. They held Pony Club camps all summer and ran clinics through the spring and fall. In winter they maintained their small band of boarders and planned for the next season.

Ortquist said, "How did they die again?"

"Blister beetles."

"What's that?"

"A bug. Toxic to horses. They were in the grain."

"You found them?"

"Bits and pieces. Not enough to prove anything, but that's what happened all the same."

"Silas wasn't charged."

Lena said, "No, he wasn't. Like I said, we didn't find enough."

"But you're convinced."

Lena said nothing.

Ortquist took out his cell phone, muttered something to himself about the reception as he dialed a number off a business card. While he waited for an answer he handed Lena his own card, which she slipped into her pocket absently. He said into the phone, "Yes, it's Detective Ortquist. Yes." He held the phone over the Chevy's center console.

Lena said, "What's this?"

"Your son."

"You told on me?" She set the phone, hot from Ortquist's pocket, against her ear, said, "Hi, Riley."

Riley said, "Mom — Jesus fucking Christ."

"That's nice."

"Don't give me *nice*. I've been going crazy here. We're all going crazy. Are you all right?"

"I'm fine. We've been riding."

"You've been riding," he said. "You and Rain."

"Yes."

"Is she okay? Her parents are out of their minds."

Lena felt a knot of remorse throb in her gut. "She's fine. We're both fine."

He said, "What were you thinking?" She would not have tolerated the paternalistic tone from her son but for the fact that she knew he was at least a bit justified. She was sure he had been sick with worry. Rain's parents as well. They were all decent people,

all well meaning, and none of them, she was certain, had the capacity to understand what she was doing.

"I'm coming to get you," Riley said in response to her silence.
"You're going to get yourself killed out there and I'm not losing
another parent this week. Put the cop back on the phone."

Ortquist told Riley where they were as best he could, given
that they seemed to be slightly north of nowhere. Lena and Ortquist sat in silence for a good minute. Then Lena said, "I haven't
done anything wrong. I haven't broken any laws. I am a free citi-
zen traveling through public land. You have no right to keep me
here."

"Your son says he's bringing a trailer for the horses."

"I'm not trailering my horse."

Ortquist said quietly, "Your husband's funeral is tomorrow.
Go home. Go say goodbye."

Her resolve had flagged on the phone with Riley, but it re-
bounded at the thought of going home to bury Frank without
having found his brother. She was not done yet.

"You open this door right now," she said.

Ortquist breathed, said, "All right."

Outside, Ortquist caught up to her. "Tell me this one thing
and you can go. Why now? If it was Silas, why did he do it now?"

Lena stopped. "I don't know," she said. And she wasn't lying.
She didn't know why now, after all these years. If the occasion
arose, she would ask him, demand an explanation. She wanted
that. She wanted to understand. But if it came to it, she'd just
shoot the son of a bitch.

She stepped toward Rain and said, "Mount up, girl. We're
riding."

ELEVEN

HE'D gotten little sleep out there in the cold by the time the sun lightened the early-morning sky to the east. He did his best to shake off the exhaustion that filled his body like marbles and chided himself for momentarily indulging in a half measure of despair over all he'd lost in the past few days—his stable, his money, his bed, the woman he'd been seeing. And in this state of weariness, he allowed himself to admit, for the first time, that he despaired over losing Frank. He attempted to shake this thought loose from the moorings of his consciousness. He stood. He ran a hand over Disco's neck and she let go a long breath of sad resignation. Silas said, "Sorry, girl."

He tucked his pistol into his boot and led Disco through the dark to the field for her meager breakfast, then back to the fire road for some easy walking, the whole while keeping eyes and ears on the sky, waiting for the return of the chopper.

It didn't take long. The sun was up now and they'd made it a few miles, maybe five, when the machine's whirring sent them back under the cover of the trees, at which point movement slowed. But even though they were closer than Silas would have liked, the police still seemed to underestimate how much ground a horse could manage, and the helicopter stayed in tight circles, not venturing too far out from where they'd been the day before. Meanwhile, Silas and his horse inched away, quietly, invisibly.

By midday he could not hear the helicopters at all, nor any sirens. Trees towered above and crowded out the sky. This was true wild. Every once in a while, a break in the timber would open up a vista so magnificent that Silas was temporarily distracted from his hunger and exhaustion. There was still beauty in this world, no doubt about that, and it almost seemed unfair to have so much of it in California.

Silas steered Disco around a bend, and through the bower he spied a clearing in the basin below. Not just a clearing — a road. His eyes followed the road to a larger gap in the woods. Buildings. At least three of them. Four or five, maybe. He dismounted and knelt in the dirt and watched. After a few minutes, during which he detected exactly no movement, he went to his pack, retrieved the last apple, ate half of it in three greedy bites and gave the other half to Disco, then walked farther down the road to another breach in the wood. He knelt and watched a while longer. He could see six buildings now — two brick, the others wood. Disco dozed. Silas's stomach appealed for more food, but there was nothing left. For a half hour he watched. When he finally rose up off his knees, he needed the assistance of a pine trunk. On stiff legs he walked Disco down a trail to the dusty town.

Approaching, he understood what he was seeing, though to use the words that sprang to his mind — *ghost town* — would have felt too dramatic. This small, abandoned outcropping of buildings would likely never have grown into a town. But they were here nonetheless, the remnants of the hope and work of some cluster of people long gone. Silas and Disco strode down the main road. The three wooden structures seemed to be homes. One of the brick buildings—only half built—might have been the start of a store, and the last was what looked to be a simple storage shed. Silas tossed the reins over the dilapidated banister of a house and ascended the creaking steps to a narrow, soft-floored porch. The door was busted and partly ajar, but he peered in through the window first anyway, then went in. The place was empty save for a couple broken chairs collapsed in one corner and the tattered curtains hanging from the windows. Everything wore a coating of dust—no footprints or finger marks. He went to the kitchen and opened the cabinets, but found nothing. He continued the investigation in the next two houses, which were much the same as the first in vacancy and ruin. Still, these were walls and roofs, and had it been later in the day—and a bit farther from the commotion of police—he might have stayed and tried to sleep through his hunger. He discovered a tin of smoked sardines, but the can rattled as he lifted it and he knew its contents were ancient and desiccated.

There in that deserted non-place, Silas once again heard the words *What are you doing, brother?* The despair he'd managed to toss off in the frigid predawn air just hours before now welled in him uncontrollably. He was saturated in it. He swallowed the stone in his throat. The fingers of his right hand, hanging at his side, stretched out, downward toward the boot where his gun pressed cruelly against his calf. Here was a simple solution to the problem that, up until this moment, he hadn't let his mind address directly. He'd gone years without exchanging a single word with his brother, but Frank had always been there. And now he wasn't. Silas's mind was hurled back to the days when he and Frank would ride through the great, wet, fern-strewn woods of the San Geronimo Valley, passing hours upon hours of their childhood traversing trails and trotting across streams and chucking rocks and generally being boys and brothers, trusting each other instinctually, loving each other implicitly. It was here that they would shoot their father's old revolver at trees. Silas was always the superior marksman, blowing saplings into toothpicks with single shots, while Frank had to be satisfied with pockmarking the big old redwoods, the rounds becoming lost in the thick, dense timber. In those days Silas's whole existence could be divided down the middle: on one side was Frank, on the other everything else.

Nothing ever changed in this goddamn world.

So. He could blow his own brains out. The cops would find him and the search would be called off. An ending not altogether satisfying for those following along at home, but an ending nonetheless. Or they wouldn't find him, and his body would break down, its liquids staining the floorboards, and what remained would dry and shrink until he was little different from one of the shriveled and hardened sardines clanging thunderously in the tin he held. And the mystery of Silas Van Loy would grow like a balloon before slipping the moorings of popular attention and floating up, away, out of sight. Forgotten. He wouldn't be around to give a damn.

But, he thought, *why end here?* What was this place to him? The cops would catch up to him eventually regardless of where he stood. Of this he had no doubt. And if it didn't matter which way he moved, he decided, he would go where he wanted to be. He would go to the coast.

He turned and, through the glassless window frame, saw Disco, whose black eyes blinked in the high sun. He clenched his empty hand and with the other tossed the sardine tin to the floor. Outside, he hoisted himself once again atop his mare and rode past the last two buildings to where the road unceremoniously petered out, and then on into the grass and weeds and stones of the flats surrounding the failed hamlet, and then on into the woods, where in his punchy state he felt himself dissolving into this land undefined by man or industry.

TWELVE

ON some level, she figured it didn't matter. That was how she justified not telling the police that she'd seen Silas more recently. Yet at the same time it seemed utterly crucial to her instinctual understanding of the man she was hunting. Over the past decade, they'd run across one another, of course, at shows and the odd social gathering, but they kept to their own sides of the room or arena. It got to where, after an initial registering of his presence, she could fairly well forget he was nearby. None of them—not Lena, Frank, or Silas—ever attempted contact, and this was why it was such a gut punch when, one night at Positively Fourth Street in San Rafael, he said to her, "Hello, Lena."

Two of her boarders sat across the table from her. They'd been riding all afternoon; Lena's legs and butt ached nicely, and all three women wore a pungent combination of sweat and dust and horsehair. Lena glanced up and attempted to mask the jolt of near terror that shot through her. Without a word she turned back to her friends, who tried not to let their eyes dart up to the man still standing over them.

He said, "When was the last time we talked?"

She ignored him, took a drink of her wine. She figured — as well as she could figure in this moment of disorienting anxiety — that Silas was drunk and that this was simply a new way to fuck with Frank. After all those years to now approach her and attempt a chat. Perhaps this was prelude to some novel strike. Or perhaps, she thought, the pathetic man was just that lonely.

"I guess we aren't going to be friends, then."

Lena faced him and, in a burst of uncontrollable anger and exasperation, said, "You tell me this. You tell me what the hell it is with you two. What makes you idiots so dead set on destroying each other?" It was the first time — she would realize later — that she had ever implicated Frank equally in the boys' war.

Silas watched her, his face falling, as if he was really, honestly considering the question. Then, finally, he said, "We're just brothers, I guess."

And with that Lena understood something that had eluded her through the years of the two men's feuding: that it really was all based on nothing. There had been moments — the night with the hat, the selling of Ace, the shooting, the blister beetles, as well as whatever had been done without her knowing, both before and after she'd entered the world of the Van Loys — but none of those occasions, not even when added together, fully explained the war between the brothers. Their hostility had little to do with the specifics of their past together and everything to do with bullheadedness and stupidity, with some innate male urge toward violence. Her life had been tossed about and nearly ruined too many times to count for the simple reason that she'd cleaved herself to these two raging egos. She welled with anger toward the both of them. After Silas walked away, Lena couldn't stomach another sip of her drink, and over the next few months — up to and beyond the moment of Frank's death — she had to work to tamp down a rising regret at ever having met her husband and his brother.

THIRTEEN

EVENTUALLY he found a path, a nice wide one, a hiking trail heading westward through the pines and thicket. It was good riding in the cool of the trees' shade but his hunger and fatigue could not be ignored. Nor could he escape the knowledge that Disco could not go on much longer without something substantial to fill her belly. They came by a cold stream, which abated their thirst for the moment. Silas dipped a sock in the cold water and pressed it gently against his nose, which still throbbed from where it had connected with the top of Disco's head. As they moved on, every now and again the woods opened up into a decent field of grass for the horse to eat.

Around dusk he curved a bend in the trail and was startled by the sight of a small edifice. It was square and brown and completely open on one side. He took Disco closer and soon understood it to be a hikers' shelter. Peering inside he spied two bunk-style cots and a table with three chairs. He came down from the horse and went in. The beds had no mattresses but tightly woven tarpaulins strung taut between the frames. He went back to his horse and untacked her, hung her saddle on a sturdy low branch. They found a nearby patch of grass and Silas sat while she chewed. Silas knelt and rubbed the horse's legs, trying to work out the worst of the cramping she was almost certainly enduring.

Back at the shelter, he unfurled his sleeping bag and his body fell to the surface of the bed as if drawn magnetically. He was asleep before he could consider the fact of it. In his slumber, he did not dream. Nor did his body stir from the position where it had landed, with one booted foot in mid-drag on the wood-planked floor. He slept deeply, as if drugged, and did not wake until the world was dark with night, and the sound of voices above him snapped him back to consciousness.

"Sorry, man," the voice said before Silas's eyes could get straight. When they did focus, Silas saw two men. Both young and narrow in the way young men are, but built through the shoulders. One removed his Giants cap and replaced it backward. The other arched his back to let his oversize pack drop onto one of the bunks.

"Didn't mean to wake you up." The same voice. From the mouth of the one in the ball cap.

Silas's throat emitted a noise, something like a grunt, and he let that be his response.

"We're hiking," the other boy continued. "Obviously."

"Dumb shit," Ball Cap said.

"Fuck you," the other one said, and he tossed a plastic water bottle at his friend in mock aggression.

Silas rubbed a thumb into one eye, then the other. He was disoriented and his head felt heavy, as if he were in the midst of a fever.

The boy in the ball cap said, "I'm going to take a piss." He went through the shelter's opening and curved out of sight, into the darkness of the woods. A moment later Silas heard him issue a childish shriek, then the word "Shit." He came back in, said to his friend, "There's a fucking horse out there." Then to Silas, "Is that your fucking horse?"

Silas sat up, nodded, grunted again.

The other boy said, "So are you, like, a horse rider?"

Silas ignored this. He cleared his throat and said, "Got caught a little short on rations out here. You boys got anything you can spare?"

With an eagerness that Silas, had he been in a better humor, might have found endearing, both boys opened their packs and rattled off their inventory. Silas accepted a gnarled twist of jerky and a promise for a can of beef stew once they got a fire going in the pit out front. "I'm grateful to you," Silas muttered. The salty jerky set his mouth watering and landed in his stomach like a lifesaver into the ocean. He closed his eyes and leaned back against the wall.

"So where you headed?" Ball Cap asked.

"Coast."

"Well, you're not too far now."

"No?" Silas said, opening his eyes. "Where are we? You got a map?"

Ball Cap spread the map across the table and pointed to where they were. Just thirty or so miles from the coast. A deep breath filled Silas's lungs. Too far to go tonight, but an easy jaunt for the morning. He said, "What say we gather up some wood, then, get some chow cooking."

The boys couldn't build a fire for shit, but they seemed to enjoy the act of busting sticks over their knees and under the heels of their boots, and they laughed at each other when the branches refused to give and instead knocked bruises onto their flesh. Silas took over fire duty and got the blaze roaring well enough and one of the boys looked at it and said, "Damn, bro." They popped cans of Dinty Moore and set them on the edges of the pit. Soon enough the brown tar was bubbling. Silas held his can with his sleeve and burned his mouth but kept eating until the tin was empty. One of the boys offered him another and he accepted it.

With the worst of his hunger sated, and now that he knew he was so close to the coast, Silas sank into a deeper state of repose. Barring the unexpected, he could be there by noon. Easily. And then? Then nothing. Then who cares. Hell, he was hardly the first man to feel the magnetic pull of the water, to want to go and go until the land disappeared into the impossible vastness of the ocean. People, trees, even mountains, they all paled compared with the sea's boundlessness. It made a man feel silly, the way someone's tragedy eclipses the petty irritations of everyday life. The way death comes along trailing its blackness, making even birth inconsequential. And this was what he wanted: to let his existence be utterly squashed by the colossus of nature.

The boy with the ball cap stood, went into the shelter, and returned holding a brightened phone at arm's length. He spun slowly in place.

The other said, "What are you doing, bro?"

Silas flinched. *What are you doing, brother?*

"I thought maybe we were high enough to get a signal."

"You stupid? We're in the middle of nowhere."

"There's no middle of nowhere anymore," Ball Cap said. A moment passed as the other one let this statement sink in. Then the one in the ball cap continued, "I said I'd call home. I'm going higher."

"You'll get lost."

"I won't get lost." He stepped into the woods.

Silas sat with the other one, the fire crackling between them. Silas's exhaustion prevented him from feeling any awkwardness in the situation, though it was clear from his peering around and nervous snapping of twigs that the boy felt no such ease.

"I got a cousin who rides horses," the boy said finally. "Mandy. She's like twelve or something?"

Silas nodded.

"Everything with her is horses. It was just like, when it happened, it happened a hundred and fifty percent. Boom — horses all the fucking time."

"It's like that sometimes," Silas muttered.

"You ever wonder what it is with girls and horses? Like, what's the thing with them? Girls in particular. Why they like them so much?"

"No," Silas said.

"No what?"

"No, I've never wondered about that."

A big pocket of sap popped in one of the fire logs.

"A lot of jokes you could make about it, though, right?" the boy said.

"Jokes?"

"Big thing between their legs. All that bouncing."

"You saying that about your little cousin?"

"No, I'm just saying. What people could say."

"Lot of stupid things people could say about a lot of things."

"I didn't mean anything," the boy said after a moment.

"Sure you did. You meant that riding horses is a womanish thing to do."

"No —"

"Do I seem particularly womanish to you, son?"

"No, sir."

The fire started to darken and Silas said to the boy, "Give those logs a little kick."

The boy stretched a leg out and weakly tapped at the fire with his boot. A log fell and the flames from the others flipped their heads upward.

"Do you know how powerful a horse is?" Silas said.

"Really powerful, I'd guess."

"Do you know what a hoof could do to that skull of yours?"

The boy looked at him through the fire. Silas felt energized. He could sense the boy's fear and it shot a jolt through his body.

"I've had eight of my ten fingers broken, most of them a few times," Silas said. "Got kicked in the shin when I was ten, broke my tibia clean through. Goddamn horse hardly even noticed he done it. Got thrown when I was sixteen and broke my collarbone. Dislocated my shoulder when I was nine. Fucker still pops out every now and again and I got to bang it back into place. Broke ribs on three occasions. And, see, here's the thing I want you to know—I'm a hell of a good rider. I'm the fucking best. I can outride any man or woman in this goddamn state. So if I'm the fucking best and I've been slammed around and busted up that many times, how tough do you think a rider who's just good has to be? My guess is your cousin Mandy's ten times the man you are, little girl or no."

The boy stared at him, afraid to respond in any way.

The one in the ball cap came back, turned the corner of the structure eyeing Silas. The other boy popped to his feet and whispered in his friend's ear. Ball Cap kept his eyes on Silas and said to the other one, "No, I got this," then they both slipped into the structure. Silas knew he should leave, but the idea of getting back on Disco was too dispiriting to even contemplate. The boys came back with a bottle of Jack Daniel's.

"You want a drink?" Ball Cap said.

Still seated, Silas took the bottle and a swig, handed it back. The brown liquid stung his mouth and filled his chest with a sickening heat. The adrenaline rush of his speech to the boy was now turning into something else, something like panic.

"Let's go, Wade," the other one said.

"Go?" Ball Cap—*Wade*—said playfully. "Too dark to hike now. What do you think," he said to Silas. "You think we should go?"

"I could give a shit what you boys do."

"See?" Wade said. "He wants us to stay."

Silas tried to see himself through this boy's eyes. The other one, younger, was scared of Silas, that much was clear. But this one. No, he wasn't scared of an old man sitting in the dirt, his nose busted, his clothes filthy. An old man lost and without provisions. An old man nearly crippled with exhaustion. Silas reckoned he wouldn't be scared of himself either.

"You get your phone working?" Silas said.

"I did indeed."

"Call your mother?"

Wade smiled. "I left a message. Got to check my e-mail too. Check the headlines. Local."

Silas's mind shot back to the farmhouse, that look on Maggie's face when she realized whose presence she was in—alarm, fear, something like grief. There was none of that on this boy's face. God, it was enough that Silas almost admired the kid. That youthful smugness, the invincibility. Almost.

"On second thought, it might be best if you two go ahead and move along," he said.

"Wade," the other said, an appeal.

Silas said, "You stay on the trail and you should be all right. You'll end up somewhere."

"There's bears out there, bro," Wade said.

"Bears just want to be left alone."

"No, I think we'll stick around for a little while longer."

He handed Silas the bottle again. This swig went down smoother and Silas thought of all those nights at Frank and Lena's place in San Anselmo, getting loaded, dancing.

"What's your name?" Wade said.

"What do you think my name is?"

"I think your name's Silas," Wade said, pronouncing it *Sill*-las.

His name came almost like a shock. To hear it out here in the middle of this vast night was surreal, like a dream where things both are and aren't what they should be. "*Si*las," Silas said, correcting him. "Guess maybe I should be the one who's going."

"Stick around," Wade said.

"Why would I do that?"

"Because you're wanted. Because you're a fucking murderer."

The word stuck him like the point of a knife.

"Sounds like you know everything," Silas said. "And you already called the cops, didn't you," Silas said.

Wade nodded once.

"So walk away. Listen to your friend. He doesn't want to be here. You'll get your reward. You'll have your picture in the paper."

"The paper," Wade said with a breath of a laugh.

"Wade," the other one said. "The *fuck?*"

Silas's stomach was settling. That panic rising in him mutated into hardened rage.

"Why don't you go on now?" Silas said.

"Because there's two of us and one of you," Wade said. "Because we're young and strong, and you're old and slow. And because your bag's way over there." He gestured to the shelter.

Silas sighed, dragged his heel through the dirt to raise a knee, and reached into his boot. "But my gun is right here." He pointed the pistol at the boys.

"Oh Jesus," the other one whimpered.

"Why didn't you just leave?" Silas said, rising to stand, his back and legs spasming with pain. "You could have left. You had every chance. You didn't. You made that decision and now here we are. I don't want you thinking that this is in any way my fault, what's happening here."

"We'll go," the other one said.

"What's your name?"

"Colin."

"Colin and Wade," Silas said. "It's too late for leaving, isn't it?"

"No," Wade said. "He's right. We can go. We'll walk away right now. We won't even get our stuff."

"You I don't want to hear from," Silas said to Wade. "You're a smug little shit. You annoy me. He's just a little dim, but you, you've got no respect. You say another word and I'm going to shoot you. You got that?" He thought, *I killed a man. This week, I killed a man. I could kill this boy.* He took another swig from the bottle. "You want a drink, Colin?"

"No, thank you."

"Take it. It'll steady you."

Colin held his hand out and took the bottle, spilled some into his mouth and down his chin.

"He doesn't get any," Silas said, gesturing to Wade with the gun.

"Look, mister," Wade said, and Silas pulled the trigger and buried a bullet in the boy's thigh. He collapsed to the dirt and cried out into the darkness of the woods. Colin held a hand to his mouth and stared down at his writhing, perforated friend, stunned.

The boy twisted, blood blackening the leg of his pants.

"That's what I mean," Silas said. "I said not another word but there you went, talking. It's arrogant, not bothering to follow one simple direction. Thinking you always know better."

Silas was amazed at how easy it was. Where shooting Frank had been agony, this was nothing. The act left him feeling little other than a vague desire to do it again, to put the boy's lights out for good. Because he could. Because he did not care for or about this person. Because, he knew then, his own life was over, and so what difference would it make.

He turned to Colin. "He's got to be a frustrating person to be friends with."

"We're brothers," Colin managed to say. "Fuck, please don't kill him, he's my brother."

Silas's gleeful rage faltered and he was once again consumed by a mournful exhaustion. He breathed. "Take your belt off," he said to Colin.

He let the boy tourniquet his brother's leg, an act that seemed to be appreciated on some level, and then tied both boys' hands with the straps of their bags. The cops would find them, take care of them like they needed taking care of. Deliver them to their mother, who had made them promise to call. They'd survive.

He tacked Disco and, taking the trail as fast as he could — which was not very fast at all, given the black around them and the twisting terrain underfoot — Silas kept a picture of Colin in his mind, the way the boy seemed to marvel at the situation, that anything like this could happen to them.

Disco stepped carefully through the darkness. Between the trees Silas could see an opening in the woods where the moon-light shone bright enough that they would be able to pick up speed. He didn't know where the cops would be coming from, but he figured the east. In his recollection of the boys' map, there didn't seem to be much of anything between him and the coast. They'd be on his tail, though. They were coming and he was run-ning out of land. Out of time. That was fine, he told himself. He was running out of energy too. He'd never felt so old as he did then, so old and tired. Not even the good horse beneath him could make him feel like anything but a man wandering alone through the dark. The bower overhead spread and the moon appeared but didn't make a damn bit of difference as Silas squeezed his legs into Disco's flanks.

FOURTEEN

T **HIS** is terrible," Rain said.

Lena said, "What is?" They'd crested a westward ridge and were ambling along a trail just wide enough for them to move side by side.

"I don't know how to say it. I mean, to you. With everything you're going through. And the reason we're out here—which is so insane I don't even think my brain can understand it. But I have this feeling."

After a pause, Lena said, "You going to tell me what it is?"

Rain looked over sheepishly. "It's just—I'm having fun. I know this isn't about fun. Of course. It's like, the opposite. But being out here, riding with you—I'm sore and hungry. And we have this horrible purpose. But it makes me think about how stupid so much of my life is. Does that make any sense?"

A breath of wind came across them and angled down the collar of Lena's fleece. She said nothing.

"I don't know if I've said this before," Rain said, "but you're really amazing."

"Am I."

"The way you teach and run the stable and don't take any shit.

Jesus, look what you're doing. You're like this badass lady."

Lena felt a terrible guilt overtake her. How had she let it happen, let this girl come along on this awful errand? Cowardice. Fear of doing this thing alone. Fear of being alone, full stop. This guilt wedged itself in her gut and dislodged something. She pulled back on Pepper's reins and lunged off him. "Take him," she commanded Rain. Lena dropped the reins to the ground and made for the cover of the woods, going until her bowels could be kept at bay no more.

Finished, she wiped as best she could with what was within reach, stood, buttoned her pants, and looked around her. The ground rose for a hundred yards before cresting. Halfway up, a boulder emerged from the earth. Lena strode up and took two scrambling steps onto the rock. She retrieved her phone from her pocket and turned it on for the first time since charging it in Ortquist's car. Ignoring the dozens of voicemails, she scrolled to her son's number and called. Ellipses points appeared and disappeared on the screen, connecting. She waited and nearly gave up—she'd been half hoping it wouldn't find a signal anyway— when the connection took and a garbled, broken ring sounded. Lena held the busted flip phone gently with two hands. Finally, the ringing stopped, but she heard no one on the other end.

"Hello?" she said.

Nothing.

"Hello?" again.

"Ell—"

"Riley, can you hear me?"

"Mom?" His voice was barely there, as if he were emerging from a dream.

"Yes, can you hear me?"

"— m. I —"

"Riley, if you can hear me, then just listen. I'm all right. Everything is all right, but I need you to do something. Get the keys to the truck and hook up the trailer. The tan one with the brown stripe. Get it ready and drive north. I'll call you again in a while with specifics. Can you hear me, sweetheart? I need you to do this for me."

"— ere you are . . . ailer but I —"

Lena listened for more, but nothing came. Finally the connection was lost and she closed her phone and stepped carefully down from the boulder.

When she got back to Rain and the horses she said, "It's time to part ways, Rain. You've been better company than I deserve, but you need to head home now. Loop on back to that town we saw a bit ago. Call the house and get a hold of Riley. He's getting the trailer ready. He'll pick you up. It'll take him a good few hours and I'll be well on my way. You're a good friend, but you've got to go now."

Rain watched Lena, and the two women held each other's gaze for several long moments before Rain said, "Okay."

Lena said, "Yeah?"

"Yeah, okay."

The exchange was far simpler than Lena had expected. She'd anticipated resistance, talk of loyalty, duty, sisterly solidarity. She had to admit that, in some ways, she'd wanted something of a protest, for Rain to argue with her like she had the day before. But now the girl casually handed Pepper's reins over to Lena. They each mounted and Lena turned in the saddle, said, "You've got the number at the house."

"Of course," Rain said.

"I appreciate your friendship, Rain. I really do. More than I can say."

Rain said, "Me too," in a quick tone Lena could not quite read, but then the girl offered a small, sad smile. Lena's heart sank at the prospect of never seeing this girl again, for of course this was a possibility, no matter how successful Lena had been in pushing this scenario from her consciousness. The surety that had consumed her in the initial chapters of this ghastly quest had waned over the course of the hours and days and countless miles they'd ridden, leaving room for doubt to encroach and pollute her resolve. Yet she rode away and rode on. She did not look behind her to see her young friend turn a corner, out of sight. Rather, she focused herself forward, listening for the sound of sirens, footsteps, traffic, waves. She felt like an animal, alert to both predators and prey. It was a terrible, terrible feeling.

More than an hour had passed when she heard a whinny issue from someplace behind her on the trail. She stopped a moment, listened, but heard nothing else. Pepper snorted and Lena jumped at the sound. She stroked his neck, letting the warmth of his body travel up into her hand. She felt him breathing under her, and the expanding and contracting of his colossal lungs was as calming as a sedative. She had just about convinced herself that she'd imagined the noise when she heard it again. She took up the reins, pressed Pepper on into a trot and then into a careful canter across the rough terrain. If there was someone behind her, she wanted to add some distance. She took her horse through an opening in the thicket on the right, leaning down to clear the branches. They ascended a shallow incline, weaving through the arbor, until Lena thought she would be out of sight of anyone passing. There she dismounted and let Pepper tear at the low foliage. For twenty minutes Lena sat at a narrow aperture through which she could see the trail. Finally a figure passed. Rain. Lena felt herself saturated with anger and relief and gratitude. She knew that Rain was coming back to help, that she had never intended to leave, and that that was why it had been such a simple task to get rid of her. Lena wanted the girl gone, safe. She wanted to finish this mission alone. But she also wanted companionship, someone to distract her from the horrible grief that had saturated her entire being. She knew she could not have both.

She scoped a path through the woods above the trail where she could follow and watch, hoping to keep an eye on Rain and at the same time hoping Rain would see that Lena was no longer in front of her, give up, and head back to that town where Riley could retrieve her. Steering Pepper around the trees and brambles, she lost the trail often but was able to catch up with it enough to keep tabs on her ward. Soon, though, the makeshift pathway became impenetrable — farther up the hill looked even worse — and Lena was forced to backtrack and descend to the trail. She prayed for a straightaway stretch where she might catch a glimpse of Rain, but on these winding, undulating paths, a direct way would not come.

FIFTEEN

THE woman's name was Stephanie Coats. He met her at a tasting in Sausalito and they got to talking over a passable Sonoma Merlot. She came out to the stable the next week and he gave her a lesson, her first time on a horse. Silas liked her so he put her on Disco, who took her around the ring at an easy, loping walk and then, after a couple loops, at a slow trot.

"When you're ready I want you to lift your hands up off the saddle," Silas instructed as he turned gradually in place in the center of the arena. "Just hang on to the reins like I showed you. Get your hands like you're holding two mugs. Now let that bounce under your seat stand you up in the stirrups a bit. And then down again. That's it. That's posting. You go with her stride, don't fight against it. There you go. Up and down, up and down. Simple."

"I'm really high up," Stephanie said with a breath of nervous laughter.

"She's a big girl, but she won't let you fall. Trust her. She knows you don't know what you're doing."

Stephanie shot Silas a sideways look, a little go-fuck-yourself squint.

"Eyes front, woman," Silas said.

A few days later they went out to Point Reyes for dinner, ate oysters and pork belly, drank a bottle of Zinfandel, then wandered the dunes until dark. Riding didn't seem to thrill her, and Silas was surprised that this indifference to the sport he'd devoted his life to made him all the more attracted to her. She listened to his horse stories, both recent and long past, not because she cared so much about the dangers and pleasures of riding or about the intricate politics of the equestrian world but because—Silas thought—she liked him too. Stephanie was funny. Good-looking and smart and funny. He'd been with countless women, and few had made him feel so comfortable. Faint praise, perhaps, but he was getting older, and "comfortable" no longer felt like a betrayal of his principles. Were anger and ambition the virtues he'd always held them to be? Stephanie was a good woman who liked to smile. She enjoyed wine and sex. She didn't ruminate on her past—not out loud, anyway—and seemed to look forward to the morning. Silas admired her.

He could not sleep, though, the nights Stephanie stayed over. He figured he was too old to learn to sleep with someone in his bed, too old not to be disturbed by the heat and movement of another body. Plus, it was a damn small bed in that old trailer. Still, he enjoyed having her there—not just for the sex, which was slow and long and undeniably good, but also for the company. He might have been too old to learn to slumber with an arm flung across his chest, but he was also too old to happily accept night after night of solitude. Television bored him and he rarely turned his on. Books put him to sleep even when he wasn't tired. A game of solitaire was too sad to even contemplate. Used to be he went out to a bar, but even that had become a dreary endeavor. The crowds annoyed and even intimidated him. All that conspicuous youth on display. So most nights he found himself sitting in a chair outside the Airstream. He would build a fire in the pit out front and drink wine while looking over his land and stable. Often, when he was nearing the bottom of the first bottle, he would amble over to the barn, stroll the aisles, say hello to the horses. He'd stand in the middle of it all and inhale deeply, taking in the dust and odors of manure and alfalfa, that sweet cocktail that had been triggering his synapses like a drug since he was born.

On perhaps their sixth or seventh evening together, Stephanie and Silas left the wine bar early, before the crowds, barely past eight, and she followed him back to the stable, into his trailer, as had become their habit. After another hour of sipping, they made love in a tender fashion. In the middle of the act, Silas found himself thinking something that surprised him: he might marry this woman.

After, Stephanie got up from bed, seemingly unbothered by her nakedness, and said, "You need a drink, cowboy?"

Silas nodded and she poured the rest of a bottle into the glasses they'd been using a half hour before. Then, in a sudden, alarmed movement, she dropped to the floor. "There's someone outside," she whispered, crouched beneath the window. "There's someone out there," she said again.

The words sent a shot of adrenaline through Silas. "Probably a boarder checking on their horse," he said.

"*Right* outside," Stephanie said, still hushed. "Sitting in one of your *chairs*."

Silas got up slowly, peered out from there in the bed, but he could not get an angle. He pulled on his boxers, slipped a T-shirt over his head, and moved slowly to the window. From there he saw, indeed, a figure set down in one of his Adirondack chairs.

He couldn't see a face, but there was no mistaking the outline of the Stetson atop the man's head. Stephanie looked up from her spot beneath the window. Silas went back to the bed and retrieved her clothes. "Here," he said as quietly as he could without whispering. He wouldn't be made to whisper in his own house. While she got dressed, Silas took down his gun from the closet.

"Oh my God," Stephanie said.

"It's all right," he said.

He opened the door, waited a beat, eyes on the unmoving figure, then said, "What do you want, Frank?"

"I didn't mean to interrupt," Frank said. "I didn't know you'd have company."

"You come peeping?"

"I caught a bit of her in the window, I'm afraid. Turned away as fast as I could. Please apologize to her if I gave her a fright." He still hadn't looked at Silas, still had his eyes on the stable grounds.

"What are you doing here?"

"Wondering if we might talk."

Silas went in and let the door shut. Back in the trailer, Stephanie was dressed. "Who is that?" she whispered.

"Nobody," Silas said. "But I got to deal with it. Mind if we say good night?"

"Silas, this doesn't seem right."

A good woman. If Silas hadn't understood that before, he did then. He assured her that nothing was the matter. Then he put on his jeans and tossed on a white button-down. While Stephanie busied herself slipping on her shoes, Silas fingered the gun safety, made sure it was in place, then tucked the pistol into the back of his jeans. He wasn't coming empty-handed to any brotherly dialogue. He held the door open for Stephanie and walked between her and the spot where Frank still sat. At her car, she got in and Silas leaned down to the open window. "Call me later," she said.

Silas couldn't help but grin, even with the long shadow of his brother looming. She went off down the dirt drive, leaving a gritty mist in the lights of the stable and paddocks. Silas transferred the gun to the front of his pants and left his shirt untucked and hanging at his sides.

When Silas got back to the trailer, Frank said, "It's good to see you, brother."

"I doubt that."

"Well," Frank said.

The night had turned cold with a heavy wetness hanging in its air. "You staying long?" Silas said.

"I don't know," Frank said. "I guess it depends on a whole lot of things."

"I'm asking 'cause if you are, I'll put a fire up."

Frank nodded and put out an open hand, palm up, to say, *Go on, then.*

Silas tossed a few logs atop one another, jammed some kindling beneath the mess, and lit them. The flame went out and he blew it back to life twice before it finally took. Kneeling there in the cracked earth, he felt embarrassed by how sloppily the fire caught. Then he felt angry at Frank for being there to bring this emotion to the surface and he felt disgust with himself for being so susceptible to his brother's gaze. After all these years.

Silas stood and for a moment let his body accept the heat of the fire.

Frank said, "Drink?"

"What is this, Frank?"

"This is nice out here. This spread." Frank turned in his chair and motioned to the hills beyond the creek. "All that yours too?"

"You know it is." He went inside and brought out a bottle of cab and two stout, stemless glasses. Poured each a good amount.

"She something special, that woman?"

"Goddamn it, Frank, you and I ain't friends."

Frank nodded in agreement. "Just brothers," he said. He took a drink. "I'm unarmed," he said. "In case you want to take your balls out of harm's way."

Silas removed the gun, sat down, and set the weapon on the arm of the chair, pointed in Frank's direction. "Better?" he said.

Frank started to say something, then paused and lifted his back off the chair and sat again. "That's maybe just what I came to talk to you about."

"What's that?"

Frank drained his glass and held the empty out. Silas watched him a beat, then took the bottle from where he'd set it in the dirt, filled his brother's glass. Frank took a drink and pulled a cigarette from a pack in his shirt pocket. He lit it with a Zippo and took a short drag.

"You still doing that?"

"Don't matter," Frank said, exhaling. In the faint light of the trailer window, smoke rose from his brother's mouth and disappeared in the night.

"What don't matter?"

Frank cleared his throat and took another drag. "I got it," he said. "I got it like Daddy had it. Lungs corrupted all to hell."

Silas felt his own lungs contract. "Fuck you," he said. "You come around here looking for sympathy. After all you done to me."

"You done some doing yourself."

"Go home to your wife if you want someone to cry for you."

"Lena doesn't know," Frank said. "Nobody knows except you."

Silas took a drink. His brother was watching the stable. Silas tried to figure this all out, what Frank was up to. "So why are you telling me?" he said.

"Do you remember Daddy going through it?"

"'Course I do."

"I don't want that."

"Who would."

"Goddamn mess," Frank said. "Was all I could do to force myself to go up there to see him every few days. See him wasting away. Toward the end, I couldn't go up at all. Just stopped. That was a weakness on my part. But goddamn if this disease isn't the mother bitch of them all."

"That was a long time ago. They got new treatments probably."

"They got fuck-all," Frank said. He took a drink. "Anyway, it's too far along. They're giving me six, seven months. They say it's a ten percent chance I'll be here a year from now."

"Fuck do they know," Silas said.

"Enough," Frank said. "I feel it. It's this strange sensation, like I'm never alone. At home. Driving in the truck, no one else with me, no one on the road, there's something there. Only thing I can come up with is it's death bearing down."

"Well, I'm sorry, Frank," Silas said, purposefully cold.

"No, you aren't," Frank said. "That's the whole point. You've been wanting to do me in for decades now. I know that because I been thinking the same about you. Why do you think I shot you?"

"You finally dropping that bullshit about the gun going off?"

"You know that gun didn't fire on its own. Shit."

Anger flooded through Silas. How had he been roped into having this conversation—*any* conversation—with this man? It was as if each second he remained in that chair he was betraying himself.

"So how about it, brother?"

"How about what?" Silas nearly shouted.

"How about you finally do it."

At these words, Silas leaped from his seat, the glass of wine dropping from his hand and breaking on the hard dirt. His heart rattled in his chest. He raised the pistol and pointed it at Frank.

"Not now," Frank said calmly.

"Why the fuck not?" Silas challenged.

"Still some things I want to do."

"Like what?"

"See my son, my grandkids. Make love to my wife a couple more times."

Silas steadied his breathing and lowered the gun. "You're full of shit. This is some kind of trap."

"You think I'm trying to trick you into shooting me?"

"This is some kind of entrapment."

"I assure you it isn't."

"You want me to, what, kill you?"

"I already told you, I don't want to go through what Daddy went through. I don't want Lena taking care of me while I become more and more useless. Shitting myself. Puking all over the goddamn place. Moaning in pain. Then one day maybe she walks in and I don't know who the hell she is. Who my boy is. Or his kids. That's not going to happen. We left Lena holding the bag with Daddy. That was enough."

Frank leaned forward and snuffed his cigarette out on the bottom of his boot. He remained bent over in that chair for a good few seconds. Silas could see his brother struggling for breath.

"I don't give a shit how you do it," Frank said, "though I'd prefer quick and painless."

"After which I get sent to jail for the rest of my life."

Frank sat erect. "You're smart. You can think up some way to get away with it, can't you?"

"I never heard you call me smart before, Frank. Lots of other things, but never smart."

Frank took a drink.

"Why don't you just do it yourself?" Silas said.

"And leave my wife and kid to deal with that for the rest of their lives, asking, Why, why, why? Anyway, I don't think I could. I don't have that in me. Plus I figure this is a way to finally make us square, you and I."

"That's some fucked-up logic."

"We got a fucked-up relationship, Silas, or didn't you notice."

"You put that moldy feed up in my loft?"

Frank laughed. "All those years ago? Goddamn right I did. I'm also the one who got you audited that one time. One phone call. You didn't know that, did you?" Frank drank the last of his wine and held the glass out. Silas refilled it, then drank from the bottle. Frank said, "You put those blister beetles in our grain?"

"I'm not saying word one about that or anything else," Silas said.

Frank grinned. "It's okay. I know it was you. That almost put us under." Frank leaned forward, elbows on knees, and looked at Silas for what seemed like the first time. "This is what it's all been aiming toward, brother. All these years, all that shit. You do this and it's over, and you get to win."

Frank stood, swigged his glass of wine, and said, "If I see it coming from too far off I'm liable to try and stop it. That's just animal instincts, I'd guess. So let me know if you're not going to do it. Otherwise, don't tell me shit." He took a few steps toward his truck, then turned. He said, "I thought maybe you were going to ask me for my hat. Like that night. Test me, see how much I meant it."

Silas said, "I got my own fuckin' hat."

Frank smiled in the firelight and walked to his car and drove off into the deep darkness of the night.

Silas rode on, hungry, tired, his legs and ass aching, his shoulders and neck stiff from the wretched cold, his head throbbing from dehydration and the lingering effects of the whiskey he'd taken off the boys and continued to drink until the bottle was empty. Pushing forward, Silas thought of what he'd said to that Maggie woman back at the llama outfit. They'd been nothing but kind to him and he'd repaid them with an attack. And a stupid one at that. He'd rather have left a gentleman, maybe even something like a friend. He didn't have many of those, and he'd forgotten the feeling of camaraderie. These thoughts occurred to him with a coloring of amusement, that in his life this was what he felt bad about. Being rude to a stranger. In one way or another, he could justify most everything he'd done over the years—even shooting the boy's thigh just hours before. What he'd said to Maggie, though, had been an act of simple meanness, and he did not want to think of himself as that brand of man. But perhaps that was exactly the man he was.

He rode on until the jagged mountains morphed into easy-rolling hills, until the sun was just peeking over those hills behind him, until he spied the coastal fog bank hanging squat in the distant sky, until he could smell the fishy wind and hear the aberrant whooshing of cars down 101. When he got to the road, holding Disco back in the trees, out of sight, the traffic struck him as a sort of pollution. Behind him was a great swath of forest, and not far ahead was the sea, but between the two was this toxic, lethal strip. He waited for a quartet of vehicles to pass from the left, then urged Disco forward, and she trotted across the pavement and down the embankment on the other side. When they finally found something like a trail that seemed to meander westward, when the noise of the cars was fading and he thought he might hear the first elemental crash of waves in the distance, Silas said to his horse, "All right. Let's get there already."

SIXTEEN

LENA knew something was wrong. Jesus, of course she knew. She also knew Frank was keeping it from her. She saw him in the evenings moving gingerly from room to room, exhausted beyond what would be acceptable for a healthy man of his age. One night he made a blathering excuse to head out to the barn in the dark of the post-twilight. Checking the farrier's job on one of the school horses. Nothing that couldn't wait till morning. And then she watched him double over halfway across the field. Coughing. That goddamn incessant cough that he waved off as a chest cold, allergies, anything. "It's nothing," he'd say, and she'd accepted that for far too long, wanting it to be the truth.

Why hadn't she said anything? Pressed the issue? Anger, she would understand later, an anger born the night she spoke to Silas at the bar in San Rafael, one that lingered long after. A fog of resentment so impenetrable that it wouldn't allow her mind to acknowledge what was right in front of her. But she finally found the limits of her self-delusion. One evening just past dusk. Dinner table. It was nothing in particular, just the nagging, undeniable knowledge that he was truly sick and that the past was nothing but prologue to the present. And in the present, she loved her husband.

She told him, "I don't know if I'd rather you've been to the doctor and don't want to tell me what he said or you're so dense you can't recognize this as a doctor-worthy ailment."

"It's nothing," he said, eyes on his plate, though he'd eaten little.

She said, "There might be a fool in this room, husband, but it isn't me."

And so he told her, came clean, and the news came down like a crushing weight atop her. For a moment she thought he was exaggerating the diagnosis until she remembered that this was Frank, who seemed never to have exaggerated a thing in his life. Understated everything, that man.

"You'll get whatever you need. Second opinions. These doctors aren't gods. They don't know everything. And you'll get all the treatments."

"Treatments," he said.

"Don't, Frank. Don't give me the stoic business. None of that cowboy shit. This isn't just about you."

"And yet they're my lungs."

"And they're inside my husband. Riley's father. The twins' grandpa. This is what we pay insurance for. And if they fuck us over, we'll sell the horses. We'll sell the barn."

"We're not selling the barn."

"And I'm not losing you. Not for nothing. And you're done with those cigarettes right now. I can't believe you've still been at that. You'll get on the treatments. Whatever the doctors say. I'll take over your students. That way you know you'll get them back when you're better. You'll rest. I don't care. Jesus Christ, Frank, how could you not tell me? How could you not let me help you?"

He took a drink of water, said, "Okay. But I'm having one last smoke." He got up and headed to the door. Lena watched him through the window, burning his Marlboro down to the filter and eyeing the darkened barn across the way.

They decided not to tell any of their friends or business acquaintances until they understood the prognosis better. And after they'd seen a second doctor, then a third, they continued in secrecy for no other reason than to tell the world would have been to confirm the disease they wanted so badly to deny. They'd set a date to tell Riley, but thanks to Silas, Frank did not make it that long.

The morning of his death, Frank insisted on driving up to Sebastopol to see a horse, cancer be damned. Lena had argued against the plan, but she had other tasks to handle that day. A pair of stalls had been empty for two months already, and that had taken a toll on their business and budget. Now a couple of potential boarders were set to come by that afternoon to check out the stable. That income was crucial and no disease changed the fact that the feed supplier needed to be paid, along with AT&T, PG&E, and the rest of them.

The sun still slept below the horizon. Lena was just rising, but Frank had been up for a while, had showered and dressed. He stood silhouetted by the light of the bathroom, his figure distorted further by the sleep lingering in Lena's eyes. They restated what each already knew, that these boarders would be great for the stable, that the money would relieve certain financial tensions. Then Frank muttered, "All right," his customary signal that he'd said all he needed to say. Later, as she rode and rode with nothing to do but remember, Lena thought with regret of the banality of the dialogue. She wondered if the particulars of their last exchange would drift from her memory. She supposed that the conversation was still fresh in her mind in part because, despite the horrible event that closely followed it and this journey of hers as a result, she knew that she still needed to fill those stalls. The world does not stop.

Did Frank's short time left on the earth change the nature of the crime committed against him? Did it change anything when the murdered man was in the process of dying anyway? She asked herself the question once, at the hospital, just after confirming that her husband was in fact gone, and then decided easily that, no, it didn't change a goddamn thing.

❧

She slept the night alone. At dawn she ate a granola bar and drank a small ration of water. Pepper got some June grass in his belly and Lena apologized as she once again set the saddle on his back. She didn't know how much longer either she or her horse could go on.

She came upon Highway 101, with its rush of cars, the violence of which Lena seemed to understand in that moment as she never had before. The road curved severely in both directions and she took Pepper north, hoping to find a safer spot to cross. The clouds here by the coast were low and gray as ash. The land and the pavement were wet, so different from the hundreds of miles of dry dirt and brittle brush she'd just navigated.

Up a ways, she pulled Pepper to a halt. In front of her a hundred yards was an orange VW Bug stopped at the side of the road. A young woman, maybe thirty, with brown hair pulled back into a ponytail, sat propped up against the fender. Lena watched for a moment, then the woman turned her head and spotted Lena and Pepper. She stood up from the side of the car and raised her hand in a shy wave. Lena urged Pepper on up the road.

Approaching, Lena said, "Trouble?"

"It just stopped. And my phone's dead. Do you have one I can borrow? I don't even know if there's a signal here."

Lena retrieved her phone from a saddlebag and turned it on and held the two sides out gingerly to the woman. She had a narrow face and white, square teeth.

"Looks like you have some messages," the woman said.

Lena said, "I suspected I might."

"Not ones you want to hear, I guess?"

"Not particularly."

The woman smiled kindly, said, "I'll be quick," and took the phone carefully.

Lena let Pepper wander the roadside, the horse taking languid, loping steps in no particular direction. She allowed the horse to graze, something she wouldn't ordinarily do, not with her in the saddle and the bit in his mouth — that kind of permissiveness led to undisciplined horses. But this time, this day, she did not care. She was struck right then, for no reason she could discern, with a blast of grief. The impact centered on her stomach and sent waves thrashing in all directions, numbing her extremities just as it convulsed her heart and made her head light. She set a hand on Pepper's neck to steady herself. This was not a feeling she'd known four days prior. She remembered being away from Riley for more than a few hours, early on in his childhood. His absence, while often a relief at first, soon manifested itself as a sort of sickness. She'd once described it to Frank as being like a vitamin deficiency—something she felt in her skin, her throat. Something essential missing. But at the same time it felt completely natural, the slow separation of mother and child that would ultimately allow for the perpetuation of the species.

And she recalled her mother's passing, which came to her as a great sadness, of course—the greatest sadness she'd ever felt up until then and for a good while after—but it also carried with it a deep gratitude for the years they'd had together. Sandra went fairly quickly, but with time enough for Lena to make peace with the eventuality, and for the two women to talk, for Lena to read her passages from Wordsworth, for them to watch bad television and listen to Marvin Gaye together. Aside from Frank, Lena had never felt as close to anyone in the world. And even with Frank in the mix, there were moments over the years when Lena felt that it might not have been her husband but rather her mother who was the one great love of her life.

But this—this was altogether different. Frank's death was a cheat. It was unspeakably unnatural. Frank's death felt to Lena more like a burst organ, a hemorrhaging, a devastation so internal that no one could see it or understand its impact.

The woman called, "All done."

Lena pulled an annoyed Pepper away from the patch of clover he was tearing at and went back to the VW. She had a sudden flash of the woman who'd given her a ride to the police station that night after the fox hunt, when she had to bail her husband out of jail and when the terrible spiraling war between the Van Loy boys began in earnest. That woman had done Lena a kindness, and she never forgot it. Is that how this young woman here would remember Lena? *Oh yeah,* she would say to friends a decade later, over drinks, a meal, *my car broke down and there was a woman, a woman on a horse, a* fucking horse, *she came out of nowhere and she let me use her phone. I never even knew her name . . .*

"Another call came in," the woman said. "I'm sorry. I was on hold and it just rang twice. I was going to tell to you, but then it stopped."

"It's okay."

"I thought maybe because of the missed-calls thing you wouldn't mind."

"You were right." Lena took the phone. "Where you headed?"

The woman leaned back against the car. "Seattle."

"That where you live?"

"Yeah. I just came down to San Francisco to visit my brother. You from around here?"

"Near San Francisco."

"What a city."

"I like it."

"What are you doing out here? Looks like you're packed up for a trip."

Lena ran her fingers through Pepper's mane. "I am," she said.

"Camping?"

The woman seemed to be one of those people who concealed nothing, who spoke their minds and asked questions when it was necessary. Of course, this was all in Lena's imagination. She did not know the woman or what might or might not be lurking inside her head. Lena saw what she wanted to see, and in this woman she saw an honest person. She liked this woman's face, liked the airiness of her voice, but she felt a tremor of unjustifiable resentment. The woman knew nothing of Lena's limitless grief. She knew nothing of the decades-long war between Frank and Silas. She knew nothing of what Lena had come all this way to do.

"I'm tracking down my husband's murderer," Lena said.

The woman stared, waiting for the joke to be revealed.

Lena continued, "I had a friend with me, but I lost her, so now it's just me."

The woman said, "Your husband was really murdered?"

"Just a few days ago."

"Jesus. I'm sorry. And you know who did it?"

"I do."

"Can't you just call the cops?"

"They're after him too. Got helicopters and everything. The whole bit."

"Jesus."

"I'm just trying to get there first."

"To do what?"

"Kill him."

"That's what I was scared you were going to say."

The woman looked around her and fiddled with the door handle, which seemed to be loose. She said, "I got someone coming out to give me a jump or tow it. I appreciate the use of your phone. But to be honest, I'm pretty freaked out right now and I wouldn't mind if you moved on."

Lena said, "Of course," and she turned Pepper northward. She got maybe fifty yards before the woman called out, "Hey," and Lena found her coming up at a jog.

When she got there, the woman said, "I don't know if you're bullshitting me or what, but I'd rather risk looking like an idiot than not say something." She paused, glanced up at the trees for a moment, as if what she had to say was nested somewhere high.

Then she again set her eyes on Lena and said, "You don't have to do this. You really don't. If what you said is true, then you're not thinking right. I've lost people — not a husband and not in this kind of way, but I've lost people and I know how my thoughts got crazy. You should go home. You should listen to whatever those voicemails are and you should go home."

"Maybe I should."

An RV rumbled past them, and Lena thought about that old clichéd dream of retiring and hitting the open road. But Lena would not grow old with Frank. This understanding had come to her with regularity over the course of the days since his death. It settled on her consciousness like a bird landing again and again on a high perch. The woman in the VW was well intentioned, and in the abstract, yes, of course Lena should go home, say goodbye to her husband — whatever that meant — and in time attempt to reconstruct something like a life. But in the reality of this moment, she knew she had to continue on.

SEVENTEEN

HE thought about little else for a week. He reckoned it was
all a ruse, some twisted ploy. Yet at the same time he plot-
ted to get the thing done. He couldn't keep from it. Sitting in
the chair outside his trailer, the chair in which Frank had set his
bones just a few nights prior, or riding atop any one of his half-
dozen horses — circling the arena, or loping and galloping across
the trails cutting across his land — he tried to work out the specifics of a murder. Gun. Knife. Explosives. Poison. Push him off
a cliff. Push him off a boat. How the fuck was he supposed to get
him on a boat? Make it look like suicide. Make it look random,
a robbery. Do it himself. Outsource it. Pin it on some other sorry
son of a bitch. Plenty of folks Silas wouldn't mind getting rid of,
as long as he was at it. Other trainers. Stable owners. Fuckers who
mistakenly thought they were better than Silas Van Loy.

He amused himself, took things to extremes, burned the
whole goddamn county down, cut the tension, had a laugh,
poured another glass.

Then one night, five, six days after his talk with Frank, Silas
ran into Lena. Positively Fourth Street. Maybe seven o'clock, the

sun lingering over the western hills, back there settling imperceptibly down toward the Pacific. He'd seen his sister-in-law often
that summer, as he always did. Show season. Unavoidable. They
were in the same world. But they hadn't spoken in years, and
like a chronic pain, he had long since learned to ignore her and
Frank's presence. But now, in such proximity to her, so soon after
Frank's visit, he was left breathless. There the woman was, happy,
or relatively happy, sipping a glass of wine, not knowing that her
husband was dying or that he'd enlisted his brother-cum-rival to
help him dispense with the ensuing unpleasantries.

Or perhaps she was in on the whole sham.

Silas approached from behind, not to sneak up on the woman
but — selfishly — to avoid seeing the look of dread and revulsion
overtake her face as she saw him and understood that he was
coming to her. He could see it well enough in his mind.

He said hello to her and she turned and he watched her eyes
widen and then narrow, and then she turned back to her friends.

"When was the last time we talked?" he said, though he knew
it didn't matter and that this was a stupid thing to say. She ignored
him. In that moment he truly did want to speak with her, to talk
as he remembered them talking on that morning of the fox hunt.
He missed her, missed days spent at the old place in San Geronimo and nights at their cottage. He missed the blissful inebriation
of youth and friendship. Then a half moment later he was filled
with anger, as if it were her fault those days had passed, her fault
the brothers had declared war on each other, her fault that time
trudged on despite all. This swirl of emotion came out as a flimsy
bit of smart-assery: "I guess we aren't going to be friends, then."
He hated himself even as he said it.

Then, just as he lifted a foot to pivot away, put his full drink on the bar, and leave, Lena turned again and said, "You tell me this. You tell me what the hell it is with you two. What makes you idiots so dead set on destroying each other?"

A reasonable question, though not one Silas had any way to answer. In lieu of anything more thoughtful, and to avoid standing silent any longer than he had already, he said, "We're just brothers, I guess."

A few nights later he called Stephanie Coats and she came to his trailer. They made love and drank a glass of wine. She said, "So you going to tell me what that was all about last time I was here?"

"Wasn't planning on it."

"I almost didn't come back."

"I'm glad you did."

"I was scared shitless, you know. Who was that out there?"

Silas took a drink, luxuriating a moment in the berry notes, the slight heat precipitating through his chest. "My brother," he said. He knew he shouldn't say anything, but to have someone care enough to ask him was too much to resist. And he wanted to tell someone. He'd been wanting to since the second his conversation with Frank had ended. *My brother came to see me,* he wanted to tell a pair of ears. *He wants me to kill him.*

"We aren't close," he told Stephanie.

"I gathered as much," she said. "What did he want?"

"A favor," he said. "Nothing."

They made love again, but she couldn't stay the night, said she was meeting her son for breakfast early the next day and needed to be fresh. Silas felt a sour roiling in his gut at the thought of being left alone. He poured another glass of wine.

At her car Stephanie said, "You know, I've got a life. My job, my son. It's quiet and small but I like it, and I have to be careful about what comes into it. I don't know what this business with your brother is, but it seems off. Regular people don't have secret meetings in the middle of the night. They don't pull out a gun because their brother stopped by. Do you know what I'm saying?"

"Of course I do. You go on, sweetheart."

"I really do like you."

"I'll be seeing you around. No hard feelings."

That night he decided he would do it. He was tired. Tired of trying to figure out what was real and what wasn't. Tired of trying to come up with ways to do the deed and get away. He was tired of the past always flitting about in the ether of his mind, and, he realized, taking in the sight of his expansive landholdings, he was tired of the present, so leaden and dull. He would do it and he would leave it all behind and he would get away but not for long and that was fine by him.

Silas had heard talk that Frank was heading up to Sebastopol to preview some horse or another going up for auction the next week, and he figured his brother would leave early to get a jump on the morning traffic. Silas drank nothing the night before. He packed his saddlebags, filled his bota. He strode the aisles of his stable, the sleepy horses barely taking note of him. Then one blue roan angled her head over the stall door and Silas fetched a bag of carrots from the barn fridge. The other horses perked up at the sound of the carrot's snap and began agitating for their own midnight snack, which Silas happily provided. He fed them and rubbed them and spoke quietly of his love for them. After all these years, how he loved the whole goddamn species. At a quarter to four he tacked up Disco and led her into the trailer, already hitched to the truck out front.

Finding Frank that morning was simpler than he'd imagined. A good part of him had been hoping he wouldn't find his brother driving up Sir Francis Drake in that dumpy Ford. But he did. Coming around a curve just past Lagunitas. The night still black everywhere save for the thinnest sliver of brightening eastern sky. Silas pressed the pedal down, mindful of Disco in the back. Even with the weight of the trailer behind him, he easily overtook Frank. Then he slowed and cut diagonally across the lanes. He got out quickly, before Frank could piece it all together, and he pointed the gun. Frank's window was open and he was smoking a cigarette.

"Put the truck on the shoulder, Frank, and kill the engine."

Frank tapped an index finger on the steering wheel and closed his eyes for a moment, then eased his truck over.

"Flashers on?" Frank said.

"No," Silas said. His heart was beating wildly.

"I don't know. People cut across these lines pretty brazenly. It's an accident waiting to happen."

"That's their problem. Quit fucking around and get out and get in mine. Driver's side."

Frank dragged on his cigarette, stubbed it out in the ashtray, and lit another. "All right."

They drove, Frank smoking to the filter. Coughing into the crook of his arm. Silas saw the dirt turnoff, said, "Go down there," and pointed. Frank wheeled off the pavement and onto the canopied path. They continued in silence, slowly, the trees becoming denser on either side, the little light there had been on the road diminishing even further. The headlights swung across the ground. The trailer bounced behind them and Silas winced at every clanging of the metal body and hitch.

"You better hope for a turnaround," Frank said. But Silas wouldn't need it.

"Here," Silas said. His hands were shaking and sweating and his legs felt weak. "Get out."

He held the gun and directed his brother into the woods. They walked until they could not see the truck and trailer behind them and it was as if they were a hundred miles from anything, though from years of horseback wandering, Silas knew that these woods could open up anywhere with little warning.

It was Frank who finally spoke. "I think this is far enough." He turned and faced Silas. "Go on, now." Silas raised the gun and tried to steady his hand. Seconds passed, nearly a minute. The gun felt like an anvil.

Then Frank said, "What are you doing, brother?"

"Don't make me do this, Frank."

"I'm not making you do a thing. I'm asking you."

"There's a chance."

"This is my chance. And you been wanting to do it for years. This is what you call a win-win. Jesus, you can't even take what you want when it's handed to you? Now do it, goddamn it."

"I can't."

"I'm not going to be able to keep arguing for it much longer. This is the time. Right now." Frank stood stone-still save for the unsteady rise and fall of his chest. What chaos lived within the silence of that predawn. What dissonance rang through Silas's head. Though he couldn't have said just how, he knew that the end of his own life had begun.

Frank said, "If you've ever loved me, you'll do this."

And Silas squeezed the trigger. He'd always been a crack shot.

It was midmorning when he got to the water, the clouds suspended above in a solid slate block. To the north and the south the beach was flanked by a curving scrim of low cliffs. Sandy trails cut through the beach grass up to the higher elevations. The water came to shore in regular, nearly deafening crashes. Past that, the Pacific Ocean. "Well, fuck," Silas said to the salt air.

He dismounted, the sand collapsed beneath his feet, and a deep, satisfying ache radiated through his legs and back. A gust of wind almost pushed him over. He pulled his bota from its saddle hook and took a long drink. The wine was warm and tasted of leather. He quickly drained the last of it and felt nausea in his empty stomach. He slid Disco's saddle and saddlebags from her, revealing a back slicked with sweat. He rubbed her with a curry comb and picked her hooves clean, dumping clumps of forest dirt into the beach sand. Silas removed his boots and walked down into the surf. The pain of the cold shot through past his knees, but it served only to elevate the strange, black euphoria that had overtaken him. He sensed that he was not standing merely at the edge of a continent, but at the precipice of death itself. Here he understood that he'd defined his life in relation to his brother, first as his mentor, then as his partner, then as his rival. And no drink, no horse, no pile of money, no Stephanie Coats was ever going to replace this man who had made Silas's life a life at all. And now that he was gone, Silas was empty. His feet went numb in the icy water and he felt the grotesque bliss of nothingness.

In a stupor, he returned to Disco. The horse was his last connection to his life, his lone tether to the world. He ran his fingers over the strap of her bridle and watched Disco's jaw work around the bit. He remembered a time as a boy when he'd placed an old length of dowel rod between his teeth and pressed it back, wanting to know what it felt like for the horse. Not good. He removed her bridle.

"How's that?" he said. "You've never seen the ocean before, have you?" He gave her a slap on the rump and she trotted a few steps down the beach, then slowed to a carefree amble. Silas sat and fished his last bottle of wine out of the saddlebag in the sand, opened it, and drank. The horse made it fifty yards down, then stopped, turned, and, motionless, watched Silas. They remained there for some time—Silas had lost the capacity for counting minutes—and the horse still did not move and Silas slowly made his way through half the bottle and felt the well of emptiness within him deepen when from the end of the beach opposite Disco came another horse, another rider. Silas didn't know if he'd perhaps fallen asleep and was dreaming it, or if he'd gone ahead and died on his own and this was the other side of that mortal gate, or if maybe this was just simply happening. The horse and rider came closer and he saw that it was a woman. She wore an English helmet and dusty rust-colored chaps and jodhpur boots. She could have been just about any student he'd had over the past three decades. She brought her horse slowly to where he sat, then stopped.

"Who are you?" he said.

"Rain," the rider said.

"The fuck kind of name is that?"

"I work for Lena and Frank," she said.

Silas took a good long drink. "I knew I knew you from somewhere. This is some coincidence, isn't it."

"No," the girl said.

"No," he said. "I don't guess it is."

And then he spied the nickel pistol in her hand.

EIGHTEEN

LENA spotted them from atop a bluff just south of the beach. She knew at once it was Rain. Sweet, loyal, foolish girl. Lena retrieved Detective Ortquist's card from her jeans pocket. The man didn't pick up until the fifth ring, an eternity passing between each.

She said, "I found Silas." The connection was better than back in the woods, but it still crackled and constantly seemed about to cut off.

"Lena?"

"Yeah."

"You're with him?"

"I'm looking at him."

"Does he see you?"

"Not for the moment."

"Where are you?"

"Hard to say. On the coast. I might have seen a mile marker back at the highway, fifty maybe. Somewhere around there, I'd venture."

"Jesus, that puts you north."

"Covered some ground."

"Stay where you are. Do not approach him. Do you hear me?"

"I hear you."

"You're staying put?"

She thought she might have until he used this phrase, which made her think of a dog, beat down and obedient. *Stay.* She hung up and tucked the phone deep in the saddlebag, then exhumed her gun.

She pressed into Pepper's flanks and they took a hither-and-thither trail as fast as they could, sometimes ducking out of sight of the beach, sometimes in full view, though it seemed that neither below noticed her. She reached the beach and squeezed the horse into a canter. Moving across the sand, she began to make out the details of the scene: Rain atop Major, Silas on the ground, both with arms outstretched, guns in hand. Down the beach a horse stood naked and untethered.

Halfway there, she saw Silas take note of her. Corner of his eye. Slight twitch to the left let her know he saw her. She got to them. Major held his head high, watching Silas sidelong. Rain seemed to crumble almost imperceptibly at Lena's approach.

Lena stopped, her gun trained on the man. "Put it down."

Not looking away from Rain, he said, "Hello, Lena. You been following me all this way?"

"Lena," Rain said. Just the word, her name, and it sounded like a plea.

"Put it down, Silas, goddamn it, or I'll shoot you right here. She isn't a part of this."

"Tell that to her trigger finger."

Lena said to Rain, "Put it down, sweetheart."

"No," Rain said.

"Silas, put your goddamn gun down and then she will."

"What about you?"

"Mine's staying up for the time being."

Silas said, "Well, shit," and lowered the barrel of his own gun into the sand.

Lena said to Rain, "You go on and get out of here." Rain's gun was still up, still trembling terribly. Something awful going on inside her, Lena thought. All that adrenaline and blood rushing through. She went on, "Go on and get hold of that horse. Poor thing's liable to wander off to the highway and get blasted by some tourist."

Rain said, "Did you call the cops?" Voice quavering.

"They're on the way. I would have stayed back except for you idiots down here in a standoff. Go on, now, girl. You've done your bit."

Rain let her gun down and slipped it into her saddlebag. She looked once at Lena, who nodded, then extended a rein out, made her way along the top edge of the surf's reach.

Lena said to Silas, "Toss your gun," and he did so without care, the pistol landing silently in the dry sand ten feet away. She said, "You should be ashamed of yourself, pointing a gun at that girl."

"She pulled hers first."

"Don't be a baby. And what the hell are you thinking, letting that animal wander off, putting it in such danger?"

"Thought she could use a little freedom for once. We're all in danger."

"Aren't you a poet all of a sudden."

Silas shrugged and took a swig from a bottle of wine. Let out a laugh that wasn't a laugh at all. He said, "Look at you all the way out here. Woman, you've got a hell of an admirable grieving process."

Gulls cawed nearby, out of Lena's sightline, behind her.

"Why'd you kill my husband, Silas?"

He hesitated. Then: "It's complicated."

"It isn't. You said so yourself. You're brothers. This is just what you do to each other. What I want to know is why now."

Silas took a drink, and Lena found herself taking note of the wine's disappearance with each swallow. She raised the gun higher, made him remember it, but still he said nothing.

She said, "Here's something you don't know, you shit. He was dying. All you did was snatch a few last months from him. That's all. Your big revenge for whatever wrong you think was done to you, all for a shitty handful of weeks."

Silas stared blankly at Lena. His face did not change, did not contort or twist, did not betray any jolt of new understanding. Lena suddenly suspected that this was not a surprise to him, that perhaps somehow Silas knew of Frank's illness. Perhaps Frank told him in the moments before Silas shot him.

"I should kill you," she said.

"Guess you probably should. Isn't that what you're here for?"

"Is that what you want?" she said. "That why *you're* here?"

"I wanted to see the water."

"There's that poet again."

"Go ahead and do it, then, if you're going to do it," Silas said firmly, nearly yelling.

Her arm ached under the weight of the gun. Was this why she'd searched him out through the woods? It was what she'd told herself, told Rain, told that woman back on the highway. But here in front of her husband's murderer, she felt none of the anger she'd been counting on. In her imagining of this moment she'd figured she would simply be someone else — not Lena, not Riley's mother or her mother's daughter or even Frank's wife, but some strange and wild being capable of avenging a murder. Capable of killing a person. But she found herself there on that beach. Herself and none other. And she herself felt nothing but the deepest, most desperate sadness of her life. A sadness that eclipsed all else.

Silas said, "I'm not gonna be able to keep arguing for this for long."

"Arguing for what?" Lena said. "What are you blathering about, you old drunk?" But of course she knew. And she knew she wasn't about to shoot an unarmed man, blotto, sitting on his ass in the sand.

A commotion down the beach alighted in Lena's periphery. Rain, still on Major, had Silas's bay with a lead rope looped around her neck, but the mare was dancing away from the other horse, alternately trying to pull free of the rope and, failing at that, to turn her backside to Major.

Lena called, "Can you halter her?"

"Can't get to it," Rain yelled back.

Silas said, "Your girl needs some help."

"Shut up," Lena said.

Silas raised the bottle of wine, said, "To the hounds."

"Shut up," she said again. Rain continued to struggle to get the animals under control. Lena's plan, inasmuch as she had one, was crumbling. Not a small part of her, though, felt a relief at the business down the beach. Securing a loose horse was something she'd done a hundred times before, and the idea of the relatively simple act offered her an element of comfort in the midst of everything else. She said, "You going to run for it?" Silas just shook his head and took another drink.

"What's your horse called?"

"Disco," he said.

The surf continued to crash onto the beach as Lena dismounted, picked up Silas's gun and stashed it in her bag, then remounted and pressed Pepper into a trot. Arriving at the alarmed horse, she said, "Okay, whoa, now, Disco, settle down," in as soothing a voice as she could manage. The bay's eyes were wide and black. She tossed her head, the loop of the lead migrating up to her ears. Lena's feet landed in the soft sand and she unhooked Pepper's halter from her pack. She stepped toward Disco, but the horse was panicked something awful and she reared slightly, a warning shot. Still clutching Pepper's reins, she tried to calm the frightened bay. "Come on, sweet girl," Lena said. Disco reared again and Pepper tugged away at the reins. "Goddamn it," she said. Lena jerked at them harder than she otherwise would have and Pepper took two steps up toward his owner. Rain was bent over trying to keep the lead around Disco's neck, but Lena could see that Major was catching the fear, too, prancing in place, wanting away.

Lena backed off from Disco and yelled, "Silas, come here and calm your horse." The man hesitated like a headstrong teenager, then slowly rose. "Hurry *up!*" she shouted, and he quickened his pace slightly at the command.

Between the blasting sounds of the waves, Lena thought she heard something else, high-pitched, unnatural, rising and falling. Sirens. She didn't know if the other two heard them, but within seconds there would be no doubt. Silas neared. The handle of his pistol displayed itself at the opening of her saddlebag.

She turned back to Disco. "Come on, whoa, now," she said.

Silas got to them and approached his horse, sweet-talking all the way, getting a hand on her jaw, stroking down to her satiny lower lip, cooing, "There we are," and slipping the halter over her head, buckling it in place, easing the lead rope from behind her ears and clipping it onto the halter.

Lena breathed.

Then another sound, a violent thudding, came quick as an ambush—a helicopter from over the bluff where Lena had spotted Rain and Silas just minutes before. It lurched forward and hovered above the three people and their horses, coaxing spray up from the sea. The whirring of its blades competed with the rush of the surf, and won. Disco reared at the chaos, and Major backed away frantically. The girl tried to steady him with the reins, but Major only tossed his head against the bit. A voice issued from a speaker: "*Police* . . . remain where you are." At the sound, Major reared back, sending Rain tumbling to the ground. The thud of her body in the sand echoed in Lena's head. "Rain!" she called over the cacophony of helicopter blades and blustering surf and the sirens getting closer.

Silas, who'd been struggling to keep hold of Disco, lost a grip on the lead, and the bay turned on her back hooves and bolted eastward, away from the water and the helicopter, up across the low dunes. Lena went to mount Pepper, but not before Silas hoisted himself up onto Major and kicked the horse into motion. "No!" Rain called weakly.

"Stop!" yelled the voice from the helicopter.

Silas paid no attention and galloped along the path in the sand his own horse had set. Lena got herself on Pepper and gave chase, pressing her heels into the horse's sides and reaching forward to let the reins slacken. "Come on now!" she hollered.

Silas was a hundred yards ahead. She could not see Disco, who had overtaken the dunes and disappeared into the redwoods. The helicopter followed but lifted as they approached the trees. Lena's heart banged away in her chest. As she moved through the wood, a bolt of electric cold shot across her skin. She scanned the land ahead for holes, fallen timber. She watched Silas narrowly miss getting brained by a branch. From outside the wood she heard what she'd dreaded, car tires screeching across pavement. As the two riders emerged from the canopy of green, Silas was still far ahead, but she'd made up ground. He rode out onto 101 and cut past a handful of cars stopped in the southbound lanes, drivers and passengers gawking and holding up cell phones. Lena followed up the embankment. When Pepper clomped onto the slick pavement, his right front hoof slipped out to the side. The horse listed and Lena nearly went toppling off the saddle, but the horse righted himself and got back into stride.

Lena was almost beside Silas now, and she could see Disco in front of them, heading straight up the northbound lanes. Cars were pulled to the shoulder. Behind glass, more cavernous mouths. More phones. They were close enough to the bay that Lena could watch the end of the lead rope flitting and popping on the road surface between the horse's hooves. So focused was she that it took some moments for her to realize that not only was the helicopter hovering alongside, but police cars were now not far behind them, lights flashing. Still she rode on. She rode because she wanted to ease that horse to safety. She rode because after the events of the past days, she could think of nothing else to do.

Another half mile and Lena and Silas were within five, six lengths of the bay. Then it happened. As if in slow motion. Lena saw the end of the lead jump and land with Disco's stride, and the bay's hoof come solidly down on it. The rope went taut and jerked the horse's head down and her momentum flipped that great animal up through the air, and she landed on her back with such force that it seemed to quake the earth itself. Silas issued a thunderous exclamation of horror, a sound from deep within the man. Lena pulled Pepper's reins too hard, too quickly, and the horse's head flew up and his hooves went sliding and Lena was once again nearly flung from Pepper's back. Silas sprang from Major before the horse was stopped and was thrown into two leaping strides across the road and fell onto his hands and chest and face. He got back to his feet and ran to his downed mare.

Silas knelt at his horse. Blood streamed from his nose. Disco was on her side, alert but barely moving. Her nostrils flared and expelled thick plumes of breath. Along her spine, patches of skin had been sheared off by the asphalt. Lena dismounted and took Major's reins before he too bolted and the terrible mad dash began anew.

"Silas," Lena said, though she could think of nothing else to say to him. She wanted to point out the police, who'd stopped their vehicles in a line not a hundred feet behind them, but this detail of their situation seemed irrelevant to the scene of a rider and his horse. She wanted to kill him, her husband's murderer, but she struggled to reconcile the man who shot Frank with the one who now caressed an injured animal.

The police called through a bullhorn, told the two of them to raise their hands, to walk toward them. Lena looked back and saw they had guns drawn.

Silas said, "Don't let them put her down." His focus remained on the horse. "Whatever vets the cops bring in are going to say she needs to be put down, but don't let them. Unless she's paralyzed,

don't let them. They're lazy and they don't give a shit about her."
Then he looked up at Lena. "You'll take her? You'll do this for
me?"

"Yes," she said.

"Fuck, Lena," Silas said. "If I had it to do over." But he did not
finish the thought. He turned back to the bay. "By God but you're
a good goddamn horse."

He stood and stepped toward Lena. The cops shouted for him
to remain still. Silas didn't look at her but reached into her saddlebag and pulled out his gun.

"Oh, Silas, don't," Lena said, but he'd already marched away
from her and the horses.

EPILOGUE

LENA arrived at the stable early, just after seven o'clock. A few trailers were already being pulled into place, and riders coaxed their steeds down the ramps, rewarded them with carrots and apples. A trio of women tied their horses and gathered around the front of one's truck. A box of pastries was open on the hood. Each of the women drank from steaming silver travel mugs. Another truck and trailer arrived and eased its way down the drive. Then another. Another. Each pulled into the pall of fog that lingered yet on the field between the barn and the house. The scene was no less entrancing for its utter familiarity. It was early May. The most beautiful moments of the year were upon the region. Cool mornings and evenings. Warm days.

Lena had sold the property in January, five months after Frank's death. It was a struggle to get the deal made, but in the end, with the help of a banker Lena had known and worked with for years, a woman whose daughters had taken lessons from Frank, the stable was sold to Rain for much less than what Lena knew it was worth. No matter. The barn, the land, the house, all of them belonged to her now. And this day she was holding her inaugural show, a simple hunter-jumper affair.

Lena wouldn't participate in the event. She had developed a distaste for competition and the hullabaloo of shows. The measuring of one's skills against another's, the pinning and collecting of ribbons, it all seemed to her, if not harmful, then at least unnecessary. She'd moved Pepper and Disco to a small ten-stall barn near her new place in San Anselmo. She rode Pepper a few times a week, usually leisurely trots and canters, occasionally taking a low-set rail if the old boy had a good bit of energy to burn off. Disco couldn't be ridden due to extensive bruising to her spine, but she was a sweet-natured girl, if a bit skittish from time to time. Mostly Lena let the two of them wander and graze in the pasture. She'd sit on the fence and watch as they absently flicked their tails at flies. This was enough for her just then.

"You didn't bring Pepper?" Rain said from behind her.

"No," Lena said, turning and finding her young friend in clean britches and a crisp white shirt.

"You should have. You would have beat the pants off everybody."

Lena pressed her lips into a smile. "Another time."

Rain came to Lena and hugged her. "It isn't the same without you here."

"Well," Lena said. She took in the barn, the outdoor arena. "New judges' stand."

"It's a new fence too."

Lena said, "Ah. It is. I couldn't tell at first."

"A few other things, too. Want a walk around?"

"You must have things to do."

"Please. I'm so nervous I've had everything ready for a week now."

Rain led Lena around the arena and through the barn, where

they came to Major's stall. He was working through a flake of alfalfa but, seeing Lena, put his head over the door.

"How is he?"

"Good," Rain said. "A little jumpy. We've been taking it easy, but he's a strong boy."

Lena caressed Major's satiny chin. "This is the horse you're going to think of years from now, you know that? You're going to have a lot of them in and out of here, but this is the one you'll come back to. This is your special one."

Rain wiped tears from her cheeks. "Which was yours?"

"I still have mine."

The old barn hands, all of whom had stuck around after the sale of the stable, waved and called out to Lena. Some came to her with smiles and awkward but sincere greetings. Lena reciprocated, inquiring after family members and states of health. She knew the place and the people so well that the few changes that had occurred shone as if spotlighted: The new arena fence and judges' stand, freshly painted gates and rails and standards, three new stall doors. *Good for her,* Lena thought. Best to make some changes straightaway. Let the place know who's in charge.

Rain said, "You know you can board them here. For nothing."

Lena looked at her. "You can't afford to give stalls away. I know the numbers as well as you do."

"We could make it work."

"No," Lena said. "Anyhow, it's better this way."

They walked to the arena, where the early jumper-class riders were measuring strides between jumps and the flat classers were mounting carefully.

Rain said, "I think about being out there with you all the time. I dream about it."

"I do too."

Rain said, "I've dreamed about him. More than a few times. It was basically every night for a while there."

How many nights had Lena dreamed of Silas? How often had she thought of Frank? The questions were ludicrous. How many molecules made up the air? How many atoms locked together to construct the earth? It was all immeasurable—her past and present, her days and nights, her love and anger and grief. All of it continuous and endless.

Lena said to Rain, "You have things to do. I've headed up enough of these to know nothing's ever done completely."

"I guess there are things I could be handling."

"Go on."

With a long hug, Rain left Lena, walking businesslike around a bend of fencing. Over the next hour, the crowd grew. With few exceptions Lena knew everyone arriving, but she said little to anyone and no one said much to her. The first class started, a junior flat, just a handful of riders. Lena watched from a discreet spot at the far end of the arena as the right girl got blue. Good young rider. Good form. There was a time, not too long before, when Lena would have tried to poach her. Would have tried and succeeded. The girl would have been boarding with them before the week was up. But that was no concern of Lena's anymore. She was out of the business, happily irrelevant. The girl accepted her blue and nodded to the judges—the excitement of a win barely contained in that young face—and exited the arena trailing a low cumulus of gray dust.

A scenario ran through Lena's head: Frank lives. Well, for a while, anyway. The disease continues its march through Frank's body and eventually kills him, some night, in some hospital bed, with Lena there to cry and hold the scabbed heft of his hand. Until then, though, she has him. In his frequent agony and incoherence, but she has him. Riley comes to the hospital and whispers quiet words at his father. Even Silas shows up to see his brother off. Ill deeds are forgiven. Hatchets buried. The fraternal feud at last put to rest. Lena and Silas spend silent time together in the hospital room, in the waiting room, in some horribly bright hall between the nurses' station and the room where the warmth of Frank's body lingers yet in the polyester mattress stuffing. She looks at her brother-in-law and sees those features he shared with her husband: the longish nose, the rounded jawline — these common characteristics that Lena had remarked upon once or twice early on but that neither boy would acknowledge. Silas's mouth purses into a sad smile, and at once Lena knows that the past is the past and that sometime in the future, when the acute pain of Frank's departure has faded and all that remains is the tinnitus-like ringing of grief, she and Silas might run into each other at an event and nod and say hello and even eventually share a small, fond memory of their history. And with this, for a moment, Lena won't feel so utterly alone.

After the second class, Lena felt she'd offered sufficient support to her friend. She walked along the edge of the property beneath a line of colossal eucalyptus trees and made her way back to the far spot in the field where she'd parked Frank's truck. The door squealed as she opened it, but the truck's frame scarcely registered her small body in the driver's seat. Across the field, her old house sat squat beneath rolling shoulders of earth. The truck reeked of ancient cigarette smoke and Lena thought to herself the same words she'd been thinking for half a year, the words that she imagined would echo for years to come, regular as a mantra, useless as a prayer: *I want you back, I want you back, I want you back.*

She turned the key, and the truck's engine started with a sudden exclamation, like a man clearing his throat in a silent room. The morning's dew had yet to evaporate from the hood of the truck.

On the seat next to her was a cardboard box, her name and address printed in tidy letters across a white label. It had been Detective Ortquist who'd phoned and told her of the situation. He said that normally someone from the coroner would call but these seemed to be special circumstances. He figured it might be better coming from him, this odd question.

"What question is that," Lena had said.

"We're legally obligated to ask the next of kin," he said, "if they want the remains."

"Silas's remains."

"Yes, ma'am."

"For Christ's sake."

"Believe me, we wrestled with this," Ortquist said. "But there are no other relatives."

"And what happens if I say no?"

"There's a place they go."

"The trash."

"Not the trash," he said. "But, yes, they're disposed of."

So on the passenger seat sat a box. Inside the box was a thick plastic bag. Inside the bag was Silas.

It was while staring at that box, a nightly habit she'd taken up since its arrival at her door a month before, that she came to understand something: There'd been more to her husband's murder than bad fraternal blood. In the investigation it had come out that Frank had gone to visit Silas only a week before the shooting. There'd been a woman there, friend of Silas's, who'd given a statement. The news sank Lena for a good few weeks. The police asked if she had any idea why Frank would have been there at Silas's spread, but Lena could think of no reason. None that made any sense, anyway. But sense had never driven the brothers' interactions. So she watched the box, as if it alone could explain to her what had happened. It told her nothing, of course, but what she'd already known, that they were bonded, those brothers, in a way she'd always nearly admired. Hatred, after all, did not flare up from a void. There must have been something there in the first place. Love. Passion, even. And this was what led to Frank's death, their mutual commitment to each other over all else.

From the old stable she headed down Sir Francis Drake and up White Hill, past the rock climbers and cyclists, into the San Geronimo Valley. She wove her way through dense woods, emerged in Nicasio, and rumbled past Silas's stable, now empty and hung with signs reading FOR SALE.

She made it to the beach at Point Reyes and trudged across the dunes to a deserted water line. The wind knocked her backward a step. Above, the iron clouds were impenetrable. How this coast could be so dark, so unforgiving, yet so beautiful. At the water, she knelt and opened the box and pressed her fingertips into the plastic and pulled. She raised the bag of ashes and pebbles and shook and closed her eyes and squinched her mouth and let the wind carry the whole gray mess across the sand and back into the wild grasses until the bag was nothing but a bag and the beach was nothing but a beach. Then Lena rose and brushed the sand from her knees and made her way again to the truck's cab.

Away from the coast, the sound of the surf persisted in her ears. It was midmorning in Marin County, California. A Saturday. Beneath Lena's body, Frank's truck exhaled its guttural breaths. Cresting a ridge, Lena faced the familiar sight of overlapping hills, miles of them, already losing their springtime green, turning golden, and she wondered a moment about the vanished histories lingering invisibly in their valleys. She opened her window, breathed in the cool morning air, and caught the scent of anise. She decided then that she would get some lunch, take it out to the new barn, and spend the afternoon with her horses. Bring them some carrots, too, some apples. Lead them to the pasture and slip off their halters. Let them run.

ACKNOWLEDGMENTS

This book would not exist without the love, support, and extraordinary intelligence of my wife, Sarah Strickley. Nor would it be without our daughters, Simone and Lulu, who give me purpose each morning.

I owe unending gratitude to my agent, Richard Abate, and all at 3 Arts, and to my editor Naomi Gibbs; copyeditor Tracy Roe; and everyone at Houghton Mifflin Harcourt.

Thanks for support and encouragement are due to Cathy O'Connell, Nick Zivic, Travis Stansel, David Lando and Brooke Lando, David Mullins, Jenna Johnson, Rachel Kim, and my friends and colleagues at the University of Louisville. Thank you all.